MAKE IT RIGHT

A Novella and Eight Stories

For Anna — Thanks for being such an awesome life coach for my friend Larry.

Ron Yates

by Ron Yates

4/20/2019

Cover art and composition by Peter Abney.

Library of Congress Cataloging-in-Publication Data

Ron Yates

Make It Right: A Novella and Eight Stories

p. cm. (Ardent Writer Press -2018)   ISBN 978-1-64066-063-2 (paperback); ISBN 978-1-64066-065-6 (hardback); ISBN 978-1-64066-064-9 (eBook mobi Kindle version)

Library of Congress Control Number 2018960597

Library of Congress Subject Headings
- Fiction--Collections.
- FICTION--General.
- Short stories.
- Short stories, American.
- Short stories, American--Southern States.

BISAC Subject Headings
- FIC029000   FICTION / Short Stories (single author)
- FIC000000   FICTION / General.

CONTENTS

ACKNOWLEDGMENTS

"I Sank the Mandolin" was published in *State of the Art: KYSO Flash Anthology 2016*. "Operating Expenses" originally appeared in the spring, 2016 issue of *Serving House Journal*. "Barbecue" originally appeared in the winter, 2016 edition of *Shark Reef*. "Spooky House" originally appeared in the spring, 2015 issue of *The Oddville Press*. "Syncretism" originally appeared in the summer, 2015 issue of *The Writing Disorder*. "Shadow of Death" originally appeared in Volume 1 Issue 4 of *The Literary Nest*. The author wishes to thank the editors of these journals for publishing his work.

DEDICATION

For Ron Walton, a devoted and insightful teacher, mentor, and friend. He made a difference in my life and countless others. Without his guidance and encouragement these stories would not have been written, and the author would more than likely have ended up a beer-bellied grease monkey.

*I will lift up mine eyes unto the hills, from whence cometh my help.
My help cometh from the LORD, which made heaven and earth.
He will not suffer thy foot to be moved: he that keepeth thee will not
slumber.
Psalm 121:1-3*

MAKE IT RIGHT

Prologue

THE BOY, LIKE MOST THAT AGE, thought his father the best in the world and tagged along whenever he could. He loved riding in the old pickup with his daddy, over the ridges and washed-out dirt roads to check on trot lines set out along the river, or to the building supply store in town for lumber, screen wire, PVC pipe, or other materials for the house. Helping with chores and projects felt like being a man, and the boy loved the feeling of power that came from joining his small force with Daddy's to make things take shape. He loved to watch his father's hands at work—pressing u-joint bearings into the pickup's driveshaft, setting posts for the new back porch, or sharpening chainsaw teeth with a rat-tail file. Sometimes, though, things broke or didn't fit right. The boy had learned to fade back whenever a job began to sour in order to avoid his father's quick hands, which were likely during bad times to grab and sling, hit, or break whatever was nearby.

There had only been that one time when he had got in the way. He had been in first grade, and now the details of the broken arm—the pain of it and discomfort of wearing a cast for eight weeks—had become little more than a smear on the smooth surface of his memories, a discoloration easy to overlook. But the change in his father's face that preceded the breaking was deeply etched; he had seen it numerous times since and developed a conditioned response.

The man had worked as a roofer for the decade or so since meeting the boy's mother, but there had been slack times that required taking on other work: fixing cars, operating a backhoe, even running a chicken house for a nearby landowner until his regular hand could get out of jail. The father was willing to do whatever was necessary to provide for his family.

He and the boy's mother had married optimistically after a halting courtship. By the time Rayford got around to dating the woman who would be his wife, most of his friends were married or already divorced. She had been passed over by boys and young men because of a slight birth defect: a cleft lip repaired in infancy but noticeable nonetheless. Even though she was otherwise attractive, she never developed confidence in her appearance and had spent most of her life in the shadows. When they married, they were both past thirty.

They lived in a single-wide trailer with a rotten floor and flimsy paneling as the boy grew from an infant to a toddler. The man took on as much work as he could during this period, having promised his wife a better place. He stood by his word, and for a time the three of them were happy in the little shotgun house he had built and she had made into a home.

In her mind she had done more than her part, painting and decorating the inside, but there was only so much she could do. He had sided the house with asphalt roofing shingles, leftover bundles from various job-sites—practical, yes, but unlike anything she had ever seen in *Better Homes and Gardens*, where the featured houses all had patios, high vaulted ceilings, and granite countertops. And the property the house sat on, she finally acknowledged, was just plain ugly.

His family owned a few acres high up in the hills, with a narrow finger sloping down to the river. In order to build there, he had called on one of his old high school football teammates to bring in a Caterpillar track loader to carve out a flat spot big enough for a concrete slab foundation. This resulted in a twelve-foot high bank beside the house, bearing marks in the red clay of the loader's mechanical teeth that had exposed, in the process of chewing earth, chunks and knobs of white quartzite running in several parallel ridges like articulated dinosaur spines. It slowly dawned on the woman that these were permanent features, undisguisable except through massive expenditures of money and labor far exceeding her husband's means.

After six years in the house, the inside was still not finished. The wall studs were exposed on one side of the bathroom and the plywood underlayment remained visible in the corners of the den where the rugs she had bought at Dollar General didn't reach. The kitchen, though, was as it should be, a place that reflected her personality. In this room her husband had been attentive to her wishes. He had bought her a brand new refrigerator and microwave and installed linoleum flooring that looked like real quarry tile. In the den, also, he had made concessions: a plush sofa and a big-screen TV connected to a satellite receiver.

She gained weight over time, there in the small house. She watched daytime dramas along with lots of home and cooking shows, and each evening she prepared a big supper for her family. Her appearance didn't seem to matter much to them, but she cringed at her reflection, realizing the weight she'd gained in her face accentuated her deformed lip. In the mirror she also saw that her once svelte figure had morphed into the thick heaviness of a middle-aged woman, and she was only forty.

She wondered what Rayford thought of her. He had not indicated disapproval, but she remembered an earlier comment he'd made about a girl he'd known in school who was now "big as a cow." She remembered because he didn't talk to her much anymore, busy as he always was. And her only child didn't seem to need her affection as he once did, now that he was becoming a miniature of his father. The two of them were always off working on something, or down at the river catching fish for her to fry.

The winter months pressed the three of them into uncomfortable proximity. The man grew restless after more than thirty minutes in front of the TV. He passed the long after-supper hours tending to the wood heater, making phone calls trying to line up work, and going outside to "check on things" after donning his frayed Carhart jacket. The boy would tag along, except on the bitterest of nights when his mother insisted that he stay inside.

It was a relief when spring came, bringing longer days and more opportunities for the man and boy to burn off their restless energy. New houses were going up in the area, doctors and lawyers from Atlanta and Birmingham building vacation homes along the river and in the scenic hills. The boy was looking forward to summer while his daddy was taking on as much work as he could, eager for money to finish the screened-in porch and get new tires for the truck.

He decided it was time to strike out with his own crew. He would have to underbid his former boss and other roofing contractors to get jobs, but the thought of being in charge, advancing himself and his family, rekindled his old desire to compete. He felt as he had when he was in high school, Friday nights before football games.

His first job was a Victorian mansion, replete with wraparound porches, gables, and cupolas. He and his two helpers made good progress the first day, but on the way to work the next morning, the truck, heavily loaded with ladders, nails, and about twenty rolls of roofing felt, began to lose power on the winding mountain road. They barely made it to the job site. As his men got started rolling out the felt and nailing shingles to the steeply pitched roof, he worked under the hood to determine the problem. He doubted if he would be able to make another trip up the mountain with the truck running as poorly it was, and the tight job schedule didn't allow for any down time.

The back two cylinders weren't firing, the same as a few months before when he'd had to replace the camshaft. The problem had returned, he felt sure, because of the inferior quality of the aftermarket part he'd paid good money for at Sam's Auto Supply. The back lobes were already worn down. All that junk coming out of China now. It was a damn shame. Sam would just have to make it right. He got his men off the roof and loaded up an hour early so he'd have time to stop by Sam's store for a replacement camshaft. Tearing into the engine was a big job, but with the boy's help washing parts and scraping off old gasket material, it could be finished in time to allow a few hours sleep before daylight.

The woman was getting ready to start supper when he pulled the truck, stumbling and lurching, into the driveway and parked just outside the back door. "Come on out here, boy," he called as he raised the hood. "We got work to do."

The boy bounded through, letting the screen door slam behind him. "What is it, Daddy? What we gonna do?"

"Gotta pull this motor about halfway apart to put in a new cam. Damn junk from China Sam sold me done wore out. He made it good, though. Got one made in USA this time. Hurry up and bring the sawhorses around here and a sheet of plywood for a workbench, and bring me the big toolbox from outta the shed, and the floor jack."

As they set up their workspace and started breaking down the engine, the sun slipped, unnoticed, behind the hills. The boy, following instructions, made several trips through the kitchen for tools and supplies: scissors, a coffee can for holding nuts and bolts, twist ties for keeping wires out of the way, pencils and masking tape for labeling, and lamps to be used, after removing the shades, as drop lights. He also carried various parts, covers, and pulleys into the kitchen for cleaning in the sink, partially filled with mineral spirits. He was amazed at how his father had a solution for every problem. Finally, the old cam was ready to come out.

"Awright," the father said as he pulled the shaft carefully out the front of the dismantled engine. "Let's get a look at this thing."

The boy watched his father run his fingers over the lumps and turn the shaft every which way under the glaring makeshift lights.

The man said, "Hmph. Well I'll be damned." He carried the camshaft through the screen door, then straight to the kitchen sink.

His hands and the oily engine part were immersed in mineral spirits when his wife approached from behind.

"How long is this gon' take?" she said. "This ain't no workshop. It's supposed to be a kitchen. Ya'll got the whole place stinking like grease and gasoline. How can I cook in here?"

He answered without turning around, "Don't worry about cooking tonight. Gotta get the truck going. That's how we make a living."

"But it stinks in here and the boy—ain't none of us—had no supper."

As she spoke he was examining the lobes of the heavy shaft under the light above the sink. He used a dish towel to wipe it dry. He could see clearly there was nothing wrong with the camshaft, that he had done all that work for nothing. Probably something simple causing the engine to misfire—distributor cap or plug wires. It would be embarrassing now, returning the cam to the parts store after making a fuss to convince Sam that he had sold a faulty part. He tried to ignore his wife's voice behind him. The boy standing at his father's side sensed that the job was turning sour, that he'd better step back. Then his mother started talking louder.

"I said I'm hungry. And tomorrow's a school day. You expect your son to go to bed without supper? Can you not answer me?"

The boy saw in his father's face what was about to happen. A blankness, something horrible on the mouth. Then words—"Dammit woman!"—blurred together with his quick turning, camshaft in hand, a hard backhand motion. The lumpy steel caught the boy's mother on the right temple, and she collapsed as if a switch had been flipped, before the words forming in her throat could be uttered.

Her knees and elbows clomped against the floor like a dropped bag of canned goods. Everything was still for a moment as the boy's eyes moved from his mother, slumped on the floor, to his father, then back. He watched her face go slack, her head drop forward toward her left shoulder as her body toppled and curled into a fetal position. He could see the blue dent in the side of her head. Her bulk spread and settled against the linoleum as she breathed out her last long sigh. The boy backed up a step.

His father said, "Well, damn." He set the camshaft gently on the counter. He knelt beside her, placed two fingers against her neck, and held that position as the boy, still and silent, waited. When he finally rose he spoke in a soft rush: "Now we'll have to work even faster. We'll have to get her outta here. Gotta get that motor back together. Then we can carry her someplace where she'll never be found."

The boy backed up almost to the screen door. He could hear crickets outside.

His father motioned with his head. There was an unfamiliar tremble in the voice as it reached toward gentleness. "Come on. I need you to help me. We'll slide her into the den and roll her up in the rug."

Against a sickening gravity, the boy made one step, then another toward his parents.

His father said, "You get her ankles, I'll grab under the shoulders."

The effort of pushing out words made him shake. "Daddy, this don't seem right."

"I know it don't, Son. But stay with me. Do what I say, and by God I'll make it right."

The boy searched for, then found the trust he needed. He obeyed and worked at his father's side long into the night. The truck, at last reassembled, ran as if it understood the importance of its role. They rode over washed-out logging roads the boy had never seen. His eyes burned from fatigue and cigarette smoke as the rumbling of the engine and his father's promise reverberated inside his head.

MAKE IT RIGHT

OUR TIME—GRADUATION NIGHT! I was proud to be sitting on that field with my classmates, draped in those hot gowns, silly caps on our heads, but not as excited as I thought I'd be. The whole thing was starting to feel like something else to get through. Because of the alphabetical arrangement, I wasn't sitting near my friend Kristina, but, thankfully, my cousin Shane was seated to my left. I'd be moving out of the aisle first toward the stage—Colleen Gaines, then Shane Gaines, then the rest of us. The stands were filled with all our relatives and friends whooping and hollering. I told myself I should savor the moment, to soak it all in so I'd remember it years later. I couldn't see as much as I wanted to after we'd been marched out in two single-file lines to those rows of hard chairs borrowed from the cafeteria. Not that many of us, really, one-hundred and two to be exact. Kids I'd grown up with, young adults now. We all knew each other so well, but there were secrets among us. I was sure of this, especially when I looked at Shane.

He was one big secret. He'd stopped talking about nine years ago, after his mother went missing. I don't mean he never uttered a word. He'd talk to me because we'd always been real close, closer than brother and sister even, and he'd talk to an adult or authority figure when asked a direct question, but that was about it. He lived inside himself, a big, brooding, walking secret. Sometimes when I looked at him, like now, I was surprised at how physically strong he'd become, how much like a man. But inside was different.

Locked inside his big body was a frightened little boy who had stopped developing normally. As I glanced over I noticed the stubble on his prominent chin, the hard set of his jaw, and those beautiful blue eyes that seemed to stare at nothing.

I elbowed him in the ribs. "Hey, cuz. We'll be walking across that stage in a few minutes. How does it feel? Aren't you excited?"

His eyes did a quick shift to me then back to vacancy. "Sure."

"Whatcha wanna do after? A lot of kids are going to be celebrating tonight. I was planning to hang out with Kristina—go to a real restaurant then maybe to Conner Evans's party. You could go with us. I think Kristina would like that."

Next to Shane, Kristina was my best friend. She was our cheerleader co-captain, tiny, loud, and quick to laugh, but she had a sensitive side too. I knew she would like to have Shane come to the party. She was always asking me about him, and I think she felt challenged by his mysterious nature, thinking she could reach him and help him blossom into the full potential of manliness suggested by his physical appearance. Shane, though, would not cooperate.

"Can't," he said. "Daddy's picking me up as soon as we're done here. He wants me to go to work with him in the morning."

"You could at least go to the restaurant with us, even if you don't go to the party. We could have you home early enough."

"Nope. Daddy's up there now waiting for me. You know he don't like to spend money on stuff like restaurants." He nodded his head in the direction of the stadium seats. At least Uncle Rayford came to see his son graduate, a big step outside his normal anti-social behavior.

I said, "Shane, this is a once-in-a-lifetime event, an accomplishment. You deserve to celebrate a little. Life's not just about work."

A shadow of remorse passed over his face. "Daddy thinks it is."

I was trying to come up with a reply, getting irritated with my introverted cousin and his workaholic father when Principal Daley stepped up to the microphone to make his opening remarks. Damn, it was frustrating. I'd been trying for years to get this boy to participate, to come out of that dark closet he lived in, and he still had no friends or social life. Everything centered around that redneck father of his, the pressing needs of his roofing business, and that little house they lived in. Their only diversions were hunting and fishing—skinning deer in the fall and catfish the rest of the year.

Actually, we're all a bunch of rednecks descended from the same. Or hillbillies, that term applies also—the Eastern Alabama hills, rural and poor. My daddy, Gene, and Shane's daddy are separated in age by about eight years, but they have the same interests: working on cars and trucks, hunting and fishing, NASCAR, and SEC football. They have broken fingernails and calloused hands. Each man usually needs a haircut, and they wear jeans and boots with tee shirts in the summer and long-sleeve flannels in winter underneath their Carhart jackets. They are tough men who work hard, fear the Lord, and are committed to providing for their families. My daddy likes to laugh, play guitar, and hang out with friends on weekends. Rayford just works, never gets out, and, as a result, neither does his socially challenged son.

Shane got placed in special education classes back in elementary school because he was so unresponsive. Something happened to him when his mom went missing, but he's plenty smart. He's always passed his classes, even when he wasn't interested. I've had to prod him, but I'm proud he's made it this far. I always had high hopes for him, that with a high school diploma, he'd go on to trade school or even four-year college. I hope there will be some way for him to get out of this place. There's lots of potential in that boy. Some people, though—stupid teachers and classmates—think he's mentally retarded. I used to want to shout at them, shake them, and tell them they're the retarded ones for not seeing what should be obvious, that Shane, with love and guidance, could be a fully functional person capable of who knows what. If those idiots would open their eyes and minds, we'd all be a lot better off, but I never did yell at them because I've learned that you can't change people, especially those with little minds.

The principal's drone was reaching a stopping point. He introduced the superintendent, who made another boring speech about how blessed we all were to live in Tanner County, and the deep wellspring of human potential that was about to gush forth into a world thirsting for new ideas. How we would face hardships and challenges, but he was confident that we were prepared to meet them through the diligent work of the greatest school system in the state. Shane was starting to fidget, and we'd barely got started. I let out an audible sigh. Shane glanced at me and rolled his eyes. I winked and whispered, "Relax. We'll make it."

And of course we did. We forgot the discomfort of sweating under those gowns as soon as the last diploma was handed out and we turned our tassels from right to left. The principal barely got his closing comments in before the hollering began. We jumped up out of our seats and formed a tight, manic group near the end zone, chanting, cheering, and throwing our caps in the air. In the midst of the hugs and high-fives, I forgot about Shane for a minute or two. When I looked around, I saw him walking away from our group celebration. I also saw Rayford coming out of the stands to meet him at the exit near the opposite end zone. I shook my head in frustration but not disbelief. This kind of behavior was what I'd come to expect from them.

⁓

WHAT HAPPENED TO SHANE'S MOTHER was always a mystery, but there was plenty of speculation throughout the community. And there was an investigation. I was just a kid, but I remember it well, all the questions about what could have happened to Aunt Polly and whether or not "foul play" was involved. The search went on for months. The sheriff came to our house several times, and he even had questions for me. He was a lanky man with a flat-top haircut. His knees, elbows, and Adam's apple were prominent features. I remember a hot day when I was splashing around in the small plastic swimming pool Mom had set up for me in the front yard. My dog Ernie was in the water with me. He was a little mixed-breed terrier that Daddy called a "feist" dog. He loved to splash, play, and bite at the water.

Sheriff Anderson squatted down in the sandy spot beside the pool and asked me what I thought happened to Aunt Polly. He was smoking a cigarette and his teeth were yellow. I answered, "I think she ran away."

Ernie was barking at him, and the sheriff looked annoyed. "Why would she run away?"

I was trying to hold Ernie, to get him to stop barking. "I don't know. Maybe 'cause she was mad at Uncle Rayford."

"Really," he said over the barking. "Was she sometimes mad at your uncle? Why would she be mad?"

"I dunno. I guess 'cause he worked all the time and didn't talk much."

"Was your Uncle Rayford ever mad at her?"

"I dunno. Probably."

"Did you ever see them get mad at each other? Have a fight?"

"No. But I know married people get mad sometimes."

While Ernie squirmed, the sheriff shifted his weight to the ball of his other foot and let one knee touch the ground. "What about your cousin. Do you think Shane knows what happened to his momma? Y'all ever talk about it?"

"Not really. Shane don't like to talk much, kinda like his daddy."

He looked me square in the eyes and took a slow drag off his cigarette. Then he managed a smile. "Well, I appreciate your help, young lady. I might need to talk to you again. We're trying real hard to find your Aunt Polly, and we have to consider all the possibilities. You might remember something that could turn out to be the main clue in solving this puzzle."

About that time I heard the screen door slam. Momma had come out onto the porch to see what Ernie was barking at. She stood there looking at us. Finally she said, "Hello, Sheriff. Can I help you?"

"Hello there, Jeanette. I was just passing time with this pretty little girl you got here. She's a real sweetheart." When he stood up, I heard his knees pop between Ernie's barks. "If you've got a minute, I would like to ask you a few questions." He dropped his cigarette and ground it under his boot. A smile spread over his lips, making a thin straight line without affecting the rest of his face. "And I was hoping you might spare me a glass of iced tea. It's hotter'n blue blazes today. I expect I might've got in this pool here with your daughter if you hadn't come out when you did."

Momma answered, "Awright. Sure. Come on in." As he mounted the porch, she offered him her hand. "We appreciate you coming out," she said.

They went inside and Ernie finally stopped barking. I sat there in the warm water, holding that squirmy dog and thinking about Aunt Polly, Uncle Ray, and Shane. It was hard to understand how somebody could be laughing and talking one day and gone the next. It occurred to me that she might be dead, and I hoped she had not gone to hell. They used to come to church some but not every Sunday like we did because Shane's daddy was usually too busy working.

They had come regularly, though, as a family for a while. This started when Uncle Ray went down to the altar to get saved one Sunday morning a long time ago, right after Shane got his arm broke. We were on the first verse of "Just As I Am" when he stepped out of the pew. The preacher, holding his Bible, smiled, reached out and hugged him. They stood and talked in whispers as others began to slip out into the aisles and make their way to the altar. Soon everybody was hugging and crying. The organist continued to play, and those who weren't crying or praying kept on singing. When the preacher turned to face the congregation, one arm around Uncle Ray's shoulders, the other lifted up, everyone got quiet.

His voice boomed out: "Brothers and sisters, it is my pleasure to introduce to you a brand new babe in Christ. Our brother Rayford has come this morning to lay his sins before the cross and to ask our lord Jesus Christ to enter his heart, to cleanse him and make him a new creation. He has prayed with me the believer's prayer and would like to be baptized. By the precious blood of Jesus, he has been redeemed! Hallelujah!"

The congregation responded in a chorus of shouts: "Praise God!" "Hallelujah!" "Amen!"

This began a little revival in our family that lasted for a while. The next Sunday, Shane and I went down to the altar, and we were baptized at that evening's service with Uncle Ray. The baptism was complicated by Shane's arm being in a cast. We had to wrap it in a plastic bag so it wouldn't get wet. Our grandparents, my mom and dad, and Aunt Polly all shed tears of joy that day, and for weeks afterward Sundays were special. After morning service was over we'd all sit down to a big dinner. Aunt Polly or my momma would sometimes host, but most Sundays we ate at MawMaw's. I loved eating at our grandmother's house because she made the best desserts. Her banana pudding and peach cobbler were favorites, but sometimes she'd surprise us with blackberry cobbler, lemon meringue pie, or chocolate cake.

I don't know why life can't stay sweet, why some monstrous obstacle always has to rear its ugly head and gobble up happiness. The decline of our Sunday worship and family time started with Rayford, and his work was the problem. He either had to fix the well pump, the truck, or some neighbor's water heater. There was always a ditch to dig or a roof to repair. Even during the sweetest period of our family revival, he would be the first to get up to leave, saying something like, "Well, that sure was good, Momma, but we need to be going. I've gotta put up a scarecrow in the garden, else the crows are gonna eat up everything."

"Rayford," MawMaw would say, "that can wait. Sunday is the Lord's day, set aside as a time to rest."

He'd answer, "It don't look like no day of rest for you with all the cooking you do and dishes to wash. Besides, the Bible says when the ox is in the ditch, you need to get it out, Sunday or not." It wasn't long before nearly every Sunday presented another ox in the ditch for Rayford to wrestle with. After a while, he, Aunt Polly, and Shane were attending church only once or twice a month. The gradual decline continued for about three years. After Aunt Polly disappeared, Uncle Ray and Shane stopped attending completely. That's when everything changed. The hardest part for me was missing Shane. Besides being my cousin, he was my best friend, even back then. After his mom went missing, he and his dad withdrew into a private father-son world. Shane turned into a misfit, and Rayford's hair went from jet black to white almost overnight.

I suppose most everyone thought Rayford had something to do with his wife's disappearance. People tend to suspect the worst, but there were other possibilities— that she'd run off with a secret lover, been abducted, or just got tired and left. I think Sheriff Anderson, who'd known Rayford his whole life, wanted to find a different answer from the one people were murmuring about.

Rayford was quiet and respectable. It was hard to imagine him doing anything that would bring harm to his family. He and Polly were thought of as a happy couple, but they had no close friends. The only people who had ever witnessed how the cogs fit in their marriage were Shane, my family, and our grandparents. Shane and I lacked the experience to know whether or not a marriage was healthy. Aunt Polly's family was mostly out of the picture. Her parents, elderly and in poor health, lived on the other side of Cutnose Mountain. We didn't see them much.

It was reasonable that Sheriff Anderson would give Rayford the benefit of the doubt and at least try to believe his story. Rayford's explanation of why he hadn't reported his wife missing until the following afternoon must have been the most troublesome part for the sheriff.

He had slept on the sofa, Rayford explained, after he had finally gotten the boy to bed. The door to the bedroom he and Polly shared had been shut, and he knew that she was mad at him for working so late and bringing the greasy truck parts into the kitchen. He didn't want to disturb her sleep any more than he already had, so he slept a few hours in the den, got up just before daylight, and went to work, leaving it to his wife to get Shane up a couple of hours later and on the school bus. When he got home that afternoon, he found Shane in the house alone, crying. And that's about all Rayford offered.

It went on for months, the questioning, the searching, the uncertainty. Summer vacation provided some relief from the teachers who had been asking me and Shane questions and the kids who looked at us funny and talked behind our backs. Prayers were still offered up each Sunday morning and Wednesday evening for our family and Aunt Polly's safe return. Church ladies asked how Rayford was doing, if he needed help around the house and with taking care of Shane, even though they knew he would never accept help.

The church formed a "Find Polly" search committee and printed up posters and fliers. Pictures of my aunt were tacked up all over our town, surrounding communities, and the larger cities of Gadsden, Anniston, and Rome. The fliers eventually reached Atlanta, Birmingham, Chattanooga, and pretty much every community between.

And we were on TV. Not me personally. Mom made sure I stayed in the house whenever the camera crews came around. But several interviews of Rayford aired, featuring heartfelt responses from Mom and Dad, along with Shane's pitiful, mute face. Dad recorded one of these segments on our old VCR and we watched it several times in the months that followed. I remember how rough Rayford looked next to the TV reporter in his white shirt and tie. Rayford wore a tee-shirt. and his long wavy hair, pushed straight back, looked oily and was already turning white. His craggy face was unshaved and puffy around his red-rimmed eyes. The reporter asked, "Mr. Gaines, I'm sure our viewers would like to know your thoughts. Do you have any idea what might have happened to your wife or where she could be?"

His voice caught in his throat. "I done told you folks and I done told the sheriff and all them boys. I come home from work and she's gone. She was peeved at me for being up so late the night before. Me and my son here had some repairs to do on the truck and it took most of the night. The last time I saw her, she was going to bed. I went to sleep on the couch, a long time later, after we got done working. I didn't want to disturb my sweet Polly. I left the house about daylight, trying to be quiet. She disappeared sometime during the night I guess, maybe while we was test driving the truck, or early the next morning after I left. I wish I knew more." He trailed off and looked at the ground, then gathered himself and gazed directly into the camera. "I want her to know I'm sorry and I miss her. I want her back home with us. And I want the low-life that took her away to get what's coming to him."

Watching that video made me sorry for Uncle Ray and Shane. But I didn't worry too much about Aunt Polly. Something told me she was gone forever.

～

ON THE NIGHT OF OUR GRADUATION I left the stadium with friends. In the excitement, thoughts of Shane and his antisocial behavior faded to their usual place at the back of my mind. Shane and his situation were always with me, and random snippets of conversation, sights, smells, and sounds would often bring him to the forefront, causing me to slip loose from the moment. I used to zone out a lot. About a year after Polly disappeared, my teachers wanted me tested for ADHD. They didn't realize my attention problem had a name and he was usually seated next to me or in the room down the hall. Mom and Dad refused to have me tested out of pride, and I've since learned how to make myself focus when necessary, to tune out the noise. Shane's situation was different. When the teachers and counselors threatened to get Child Protective Services involved, Rayford gave in, and Shane has worn the special ed. label ever since. This kept us from being in many of the same classes—I eventually broke into the honors track— but even when we weren't physically close, he was near in my mind. It's been that way for so long now I can't imagine Shane's not being in my thoughts and dreams.

∼

KRISTINA ASKED ME after we got in her Honda where he was. She was incredulous at my explanation that he had gone home with his daddy because they had work to do. "What the freak!" she said. "I can't believe this guy. I've been flirting with him all semester and I finally manage to get a smile out of him, and now his psycho dad locks him back up in the closet on the biggest night of our lives. Colleen, your family is just too weird."

This coming from anybody else would have bristled me up. Kristina and I, though, had become really close. It started in the fall of our junior year after I miraculously made the cheerleading squad. Kristina, who had been cheering since she got out of diapers, tried to embarrass me into quitting but couldn't. I was stubborn enough to make sure I wasn't the worst one on the squad, at least. I've always been athletic and I'd done some gymnastics and cheerleading back in elementary school, so I was able to master my back handspring before the other new girls. That's when Ms. Lambert, the coach, and Kristina began to see potential in me. Kristina decided to take me on as her personal project, thinking I would be someone she could mold into her own image. That didn't work out. I can be stubborn sometimes, and I resist being shaped by others' expectations. But after we butted heads a few times, my mentor grew to appreciate my independent spirit, the fact that I would persist in finding my own way. I guess I've done okay, having spent my last two years of high school taking advanced classes, cheering my heart out, and hanging with the popular rich kids like Kristina.

Still, though, I sometimes felt out of place. Kristina and I come from different worlds. I understand enough about the economy and demographics to know that her family isn't rich, but they're near the top of the ladder in our neck of the woods. They have a two-story brick house in town with a real in-ground pool in the back. There's a basement her older brother has all to himself, and a two-car garage. Kristina's room upstairs has its own bath and is about half as big as our whole house.

Her parents both went to college. Her mom teaches at the elementary school and her dad is some kind of sales rep. He's gone a lot but makes good money. He got a big bonus just before Kristina's seventeenth birthday, which translated into the red Honda coupe we spend so much time in. She looks good in that car, and I don't mind being seen in it myself. Whenever we get together with friends, we always take her Honda, and she won't even let us help with gas.

She's nothing like Jennifer Muzik, the other rich girl on the cheerleading squad. Jennifer's boyfriend is Conner Evans, the guy who was throwing the graduation party. A group of popular rich kids and wannabes were always clustered around Jennifer and Conner, who weren't as generous and open with outsiders as Kristina was. They weren't exactly rude—our school wasn't like one of those teen flicks with devious alpha bitches constantly scheming to humiliate everyone who was not part of their circle—but there were boundaries. Whenever I was around Jennifer and her group, I felt a keen sense of having crossed a line, and I longed to be back in my rightful place, sitting at MawMaw's dinner table with Shane and the rest of my family, laughing and eating peach cobbler. Or helping Daddy, Uncle Ray, and Shane cut firewood. Or playing rec league softball with the girls I used to hang with.

It was okay as long as Kristina was close by. With her short, layered hair, big brown eyes, and perfect petite body she was even prettier than Jennifer. There was something about her manner—her easy laugh, the flash of her eyes, her sarcasm—that always made me feel like she appreciated me for who I was on the inside, in spite of my parent's low income and social standing. She never acted like she was better than us. She even joined us one Sunday for dinner at MawMaw's. That was when I first noticed her interest in Shane.

My grandmother was tickled to see such a little thing put away so much food. Kristina ate two helpings of field peas, macaroni and cheese, coleslaw, an extra pork chop, a big slab of buttered cornbread, and, finally, a bowl of banana pudding. Daddy teased her. "Little girl, where in the world are you putting all that? You must have a hollow leg."

MawMaw said, "You leave that child alone, Eugene. She just appreciates good home cooking."

Kristina washed down a mouthful of pudding with sweet tea. "That's right, Mr. Gaines. I don't get meals like this very often at my house. My mom's usually too tired from working with those little kids all day, and Dad's on the road a lot. We usually just eat out of a box."

Mom said, "I know how that is. There's lots of times I don't feel like cooking myself."

"Tell me about it," Daddy said. "Problem is, I always feel like eating."

We all chuckled and nodded our heads in agreement. PawPaw scraped up his last bite of pudding then felt in the bib of his overalls for his pipe tobacco. Shane looked down into his bowl.

Rayford pushed back from the table. "Got any coffee made?" he asked.

MawMaw answered, "Well, no. Didn't figure anybody would want any, warm as it is."

"You know me, Momma. I can always drink a cup of coffee."

"I'll put on a pot."

Chairs scraped against the floor as Uncle Ray and my grandparents got up. With the adults gone, we were awkward there at the table, an unlikely setting for an unlikely trio, until Kristina said, "Hey Shane, you gonna eat the rest of your pudding?"

Something like a smile swept across his face, and I think their eyes met for an instant as he pushed the bowl in her direction.

That was the spring of our junior year. They only saw each other once over the summer, that afternoon when a group of us got together out at Eason's Mill, a secluded swimming hole. Shane became even more awkward and shy than usual after we arrived and he saw Kristina and a couple of guys from school. She smiled and waved and splashed him a few times after we finally got him to go in. He had swung out on the rope swing earlier that summer when it had been just the two of us and a few younger kids, but he resisted putting himself on display in front of Kristina and the guys she was with. I think that's when she began to see him as a challenge, a mild interest that blossomed into infatuation as a result of what happened that day.

Shane wasn't trying to be a hero. After growing up in the woods and creeks with his dad, he just responded to circumstances in the only way he knew. His relationship with the natural world was on a different level from everybody else's. He saw and heard things we didn't. He and I were swimming at the deep end near the old rock dam. Billy Thornhill had followed us out there, trying to get my attention as he had been doing since middle school, but he had given up after I ignored him and climbed onto Shane's back. Billy joined Kristina and Kyle Lambert on the sandy bank. While Shane and I splashed and played, the three of them sat on their beach towels laughing, talking, and drinking beer. Kristina's feet were in the water.

It was hot that day. The surface of the mill pond was green and shadowy from the lush hardwoods and brush along the banks, but the sun poured through, making the surface sparkle wherever the water was disturbed. I was wrestling with Shane, riding his back and trying to push him under. He was a strong swimmer with good lungs. Sometimes he'd stay under for a long time before I'd feel with my feet the tightening in his lower back, the sinews of his hips and thighs. His shoulders would bulge and he'd shake me loose with a bucking motion that involved his whole body. He'd break the surface for air and I'd climb on again, laughing and shouting.

This had been going on for some time when, after gaining my hold around his upper body and tightening my legs around his trunk, I felt a sudden convulsion. My grip was broken as Shane became a torpedo, pushing me into the rock dam and propelling himself forward like an Olympian making a turn. His body undulated just under the surface, and when he broke, twenty feet away, the water rippled smoothly to indicate his speed and direction. His strong strokes were carrying him directly toward Kristina and the boys on the sandy bank.

Just before he reached them Shane's feet found bottom and his shoulders rose dripping above the surface. He'd become a predator pushing forward, left arm working for balance, right arm pulled back at his chest, ready to grab, strike, or throw. Water lapped his stomach. He pushed harder two more splashing steps before his arm uncoiled in a blur. The surface exploded in a cascade of white jewels as he yanked out something dark and writhing. His body straightened and his arm extended in a wide arc up and back so that the thing he'd pulled from the water touched the surface behind him before becoming a whip cracked with surprising force as Shane moved into shallower water. He cracked the whip again as he stepped out beside Kristina who had begun to recoil and push with her feet and hands against the wet sand.

Shane dropped his broken whip a few feet away, and from where I was I could see the thick body twitching, the head facing backwards, detached except for a sinewy strip of meat. Everything froze for a moment as we stared at Shane who stood panting, looking down at what he'd done, making sure the job was finished. Kristina and the boys were standing now, brushing themselves off, still backing away.

Billy spoke first: "Damn, dude. What the … how did you …?"

Kristina said, "Holy shit!" then dropped to her knees and began to sob.

I became frantic to get out of the water, and in my haste I forgot technique and splashed awkwardly toward my friends. When I reached the bank, the boys had regained enough composure to examine the dead snake. Kristina sobbed and shook her head. Shane stood there, looking confused about what to do next. I hugged him hard and kissed his cheek. "Way to go, cuz. That was awesome." Still shaky myself, I turned to Kristina to help her deal with the shock of what had happened.

Kyle and Billy squatted beside the snake, poking it with sticks. Kyle said, "Yep. That's a damn water moccasin all right, cotton mouth."

"Biggest one I ever saw," Billy said. He turned to Shane. "How did you know?"

Shane shrugged, looked away.

"Son-of-a-bitch woulda bit somebody sure as hell, probably Kristina. She was closest."

I didn't need to look at the snake. I could tell what it was before I got out of the water—the dark, banded body, thick in the middle, thin at the neck; the blockish head. I hated those damned things and was glad it was dead.

I squatted beside Kristina and put my arm around her. "It's okay, baby. It's dead. Shane killed it. Can't hurt nobody now."

"I don't like this place anymore," she said. "I want to go home."

She was there with Billy and Kyle, but I didn't feel like releasing her to those guys in her emotional state. I said, "Let's get out of here. You can ride with us." I turned to

Shane and noticed a look of concern, brows wrinkled, eyes darting back and forth.

"It's okay," I said. "Rayford won't have to know. We got plenty of time to get the truck back before dark."

Kristina seemed pleased at the idea of riding home with us instead of the guys she'd come with. She smiled and blinked her wet eyes. "I can buy some gas."

The boys, though, looked disappointed. Kyle, like half of the guys we knew, had a longstanding crush on Kristina; Billy was in love with me, had been for what seemed like forever. He had come today knowing I'd be there, and I was sure both boys had been fantasizing about a sexual connection at this secluded spot. Oh well, they'd just have to get over it.

Shane drove us in Rayford's truck to the fancy subdivision where Kristina lived. She sat between us. By the time we got to her house, she was relaxed, and we were laughing and recounting the details of Shane's heroism.

I got together with Kristina a couple of times toward the end of summer, but Shane could never join us. He and his dad generally worked about twelve hours a day. Our going swimming at the mill, it seems, had been a special treat Rayford offered, a way of rewarding his son for all the hard work. Deep inside him there must have been a lingering notion that young people need to have a little fun once in a while. I just wished, for Shane's sake, that his dad's compassionate side would turn up more often.

❧

SHANE NEVER GOT TO PLAY MUCH, even when we were kids. The two of us would get together occasionally, on summer evenings or Saturday afternoons, and ride our bikes on the dirt road between our houses, but we weren't allowed to venture farther than MawMaw and PawPaw's house, about a mile away where the dirt road joined the blacktopped county road. Rayford was very specific about how far Shane could go and how late he could stay out. I don't remember him ever playing at another kid's house or having friends over to his house. I had a few friends, but since we lived so far out in the sticks, and since we were poor by the other kids' standards—our classmates who lived in bigger houses and rode in newer cars—I seldom invited anyone over. I was closer to Shane and would rather be with him than with anybody else, but as special as our times together were, they weren't all sweet.

I remember the time I talked him into riding his bike with me to the round barn at the old Hudson place. This rustic structure was a famous landmark, the subject of hundreds of paintings and photographs, but to me it was a wild and abandoned place that begged to be explored, luring me with promises of the mysterious and forbidden. A tall cylindrical building, twice as big as most barns in the area, it was sided with weathered boards and topped with ancient wooden shingles. A conical roof, a few feet higher than the main roof, covered the top of a silo that the main portion of the barn wrapped around. Fifty years ago, this structure had been the center of a family-owned dairy farm. As years rolled by, it became the nostalgia-producing subject of paintings and photo prints framed in barn wood, hanging in homes and businesses all over the county, even in Georgia and Tennessee.

I had never been inside, but Daddy had. When he was a boy, the Hudsons were elderly, but still kept a few cows. MawMaw and other folks in the neighborhood bought milk from them. Daddy told me stories of going to the Hudson farm with his momma to pick up the fresh milk in gallon glass jugs. Mr. Hudson would sometimes let him tag along out to the barn as he did his chores—tending to the cows, cleaning the stalls and buckets, or getting hay down from the loft.

These experiences left deep imprints on Daddy's memory. I could tell by the way his eyes flashed, by the lilt of his voice, and by the movement of his hands when he described the architecture, the complicated carpentry, and how the afternoon sun filtered in through the cracks in the siding and gaps in the roof. He told me about the smell, that wonderful barn smell, heavy and warm. He told of old Mr. Hudson's methodical movements as he pitched the hay or shoveled out manure, and of the rats that scurried into their hiding places as they approached. Daddy also told about the obsolete, mule-drawn plows and implements scattered throughout, along with numerous halters, straps, ropes, and wicker baskets hanging everywhere. The loft, he said, besides holding hay in loose piles and bales, also contained several generations of the family's cast-off items: antique furniture, broken and dust covered, old mildewed books and National Geographic magazines, porcelain dolls with cracked faces, broken space heaters, walking sticks and leg braces, pots and pans, old-fashioned bicycles, and an assortment of outdated toys.

Of course, I was just a kid myself when Daddy shared with me these memories from his childhood. With my limited experience, it was hard to visualize all he was describing, which caused my imagination to conjure up details to fill in the gaps. The Round Barn became a mythical setting for my mind to play in, and I knew I would have to go there physically to validate my fantasies. I thought about it more and more during the time after Aunt Polly's disappearance, and in all of the scenarios I constructed, Shane was a central figure.

It was easier than I'd thought it would be to persuade him to ride along with me and Ernie on the blacktop past MawMaw's house. It seemed that he was ready for an adventure himself. The Hudson place was only another mile or so away, but to kids our age—almost eleven—it felt like a long journey, not so much because of the distance, but more so from the feeling of being out there alone on our bikes, away from grown-ups, doing what we knew we weren't supposed to be doing.

It was an early autumn Saturday with bright sun minus summer's heavy heat. Ernie was in a playful mood, the cooler air bringing out his feistiness. Along the shoulder of the blacktop remained the dried cuttings of the road crew's last mowing. The roadside had been overgrown with briars, tall weeds, and grasses. When I pulled over to make room for a vehicle approaching from behind, the spokes of my rear wheel caught some thick stalks and pulled them between the chain and sprocket, and the pedals began to spin without resistance. My momentum was soon lost. Ernie barked and made a few of his galloping lunges at the loud pickup as it sped past.

Shane, unaware, was pulling away into the distance. I called out, "Hey cuz, wait! Come back!" When he turned and saw that I'd stopped, he skidded his back tire, threw up his arms, and shook his head.

Back beside me, it only took him a second to identify the problem. He said, "Chain done come off. Bunch of trash wrapped 'round the sprocket."

"Well, you can fix it, can't you?"

"I reckon." He grabbed the bike by the frame and flipped it over so that it rested on its seat and handlebars, with wheels free to turn. As he tried to yank the stalks free from their entanglement in the rear spokes, briars ripped his hands. He wiped the blood on his jeans and with a determined expression reached for his pocket knife. He knelt beside the bike and went to work—poking, prying, cutting, and pulling at the stalks while turning the wheel for better access. His hands were soon smeared with blood and grease, and the whole process was made more difficult by Ernie, who thought Shane's kneeling that way must be an invitation to play.

He kept nipping at his ankles and pants legs. My attempts to calm the little dog only made his behavior worse. I knew the best course was to ignore him when he got into his excitable mode, and eventually he'd simmer down. It was hard, though, for Shane to ignore him, barking, growling and tugging on his britches.

I knelt, patted the ground, and tried my sweet voice: "Come on, baby. Be a good boy. Come sit by me."

He responded with a shrill bark and went back to Shane's pants. I saw the change come over my cousin's face just before he rose to his feet with a sudden energy that knocked the bike over. "Dammit, dog!" he yelled, kicking Ernie in the ribs.

The little dog was so light on his feet that the kick barely registered, serving only to make him more excited. He skittered back and forth on springy-stiff legs, barking his shrill bark, making wide semi-circles from the middle of the road back to within kicking distance from Shane.

Shane said, "Go on!" and threw a stick at him, which added fuel to the fire.

Ernie kept on skittering and barking. I called out, "Come here, Ernie, here boy." I slapped my thighs and called more urgently when I saw a truck cresting the rise a short distance away.

Ernie saw it too and seemed delighted at the developing complexity of the game. He had good timing when it came to the sport of chasing cars. He would usually make a perpendicular bee-line toward the front tire and veer off at the last minute, chasing and barking alongside the vehicle until it outdistanced him. But he had no experience with trailers pulled behind trucks, especially wide farm trailers.

The F-350 was pulling a goose-neck rig loaded with hay. Ernie made his usual run at the front tire and turned with split-second accuracy. He was in a blissful state—running alongside for a few galloping steps, barking, ears pinned back—when the trailer tire ran over him with a thump that instantly silenced his shrill voice.

The truck and trailer never slowed. Either the driver didn't know what had happened or didn't care. Shane screamed, "No! No!" and dropped to his knees in the middle of the road. I shuddered at the sight of Ernie lying there and, realizing he was beyond help, turned to Shane to offer what comfort I could. I put my hand on his shoulder and rubbed the back of his neck. He said, "It's my fault, my fault, my fault."

Poor Ernie—that little feist so full of energy and mischief, so eager to play and to aggravate—died that day, and I had to turn away from the shame and guilt in Shane's eyes over what he had done.

A miserable time followed. We went back to PawPaw's shed and got a shovel. We found a good spot for Ernie in the woods beside the road. We had to come up with a story about what happened to him since we weren't supposed to be on the blacktop in the first place. I did most of the thinking for us, Shane having dropped into his unresponsive mode. I kept telling him it would be all right, that he needed to trust me. We agreed on a simple explanation for Ernie's disappearance: We were riding on the dirt road not far from MawMaw's house. Ernie was exploring ahead of us. We heard his excited barking like he was after a rabbit. His barking got farther away. We called and called but he never came.

Momma and Daddy accepted the story. They didn't like the dog much anyway because he was so aggravating. They seemed more concerned with helping us deal with the loss rather than their own disappointment. Daddy said, "He might have gone off and found him a girlfriend somewhere. I'm sure he'll make his way back home in a few days, tired and hungry. Dogs ain't like people. They don't get lost."

Later that day I rode into town with Momma to pick up a few groceries. When we passed the spot where Ernie died, I had to suppress an urge to blurt out what had really happened. Secrets involving death and shame have a way of rising up in your throat, and for a moment I felt like I might throw up. I fought it, though, and began to feel better when I saw the round barn looming on my right, growing larger as we approached. I stared out the window as we passed by. The way it tugged at me felt even stronger than before, and I knew the time would sooner or later come when me and Shane would go inside.

∽

IT BOTHERED ME, standing there in the end zone on graduation night, that the person closest to me was walking away from the biggest event of our lives to be with his daddy—no high fives, no hearty congratulations, no hugs or socializing. I don't think he even tossed his cap into the air. Kristina and other friends were excited, ready to party. I had told my parents about our plans ... well, not completely. I mentioned the restaurant—probably the new Olive Garden over in Aaronville—and that we might go to a movie afterward, or over to Conner's house to watch DVD's on their big flat-screen. I left out the fact that the whole graduating class was likely to turn up there and the probability of drinking along with all sorts of questionable teen behavior was very high. Mom trusted me, and Daddy usually left matters concerning my behavioral limits up to her. I told them I was spending the night at Kristina's.

Before we could get away we had to extend the graduation experience a few minutes with our respective families, hugging and taking pictures. Pictures of me and my grandparents, mom and dad; pictures of me with Kristina; pictures of us together and with other friends; pictures with our caps on our heads and holding our caps and throwing our caps; pictures of us acting silly and holding our diplomas; but no pictures of Shane, except for one taken by my mom from the stands as he walked across the stage, so far away you couldn't even tell who he was. Finally Kristina said, "I guess we need to be heading out if we're going to make it to the restaurant and have time to catch a movie." After a few more hugs we slipped out of the crowd, our ears ringing with warnings and reminders from our parents to behave and be careful.

We pulled those hot gowns off in the parking lot and hopped into Kristina's car. She was all smiles. We were laughing, talking, and checking messages from our friends about when and where we were going to meet. As we got underway, weaving through the traffic, I wondered what Shane and Uncle Ray were doing. I imagined that to commemorate his son's graduation, Rayford may go as far as to splurge on a cheeseburger basket at the truck stop. Or they might have gone straight home to check on the trot lines they kept out down at the river or to get their equipment in order for the morning's work. There had never been anything I could do about Shane's circumstances, and that night was no different. I tried to push him out of my mind and to concentrate on having a good time.

"Damn," Kristina said, snaking her way into the line of cars heading for the exit. "Can you believe all these people came out to see us graduate?"

"I know, right? The biggest event in the county, and, sad to say, this will probably be the biggest event in most of our classmates' lives."

"Yeah, poor dumb losers. Stuck here in Tanner County with no hope of ever getting out."

An older man and his wife, grandparents probably, in an SUV stopped the line of traffic and motioned for Kristina to cut in. She smiled and waved like a cheerleader.

I said, "I guess most of them don't really want to get out. Probably don't give it much thought."

"Probably not," she said as she steered while fiddling with her smartphone, trying to plug it into the auxiliary jack of her car stereo. "I guess they just accept their parents' expectations and hope for the best. That's not us, though, is it?"

"Definitely not, but I still don't get how people can live one day at a time without planning for the future."

"Easy," she said as Katy Perry came blaring through the speakers. "They're easily entertained, so it seems that each moment is all that matters, especially the stoners."

"Ah yes," I said, "you're right, of course, and that accounts for a pretty big group, about half of our class."

She chuckled. "We'll get to see most of them tonight, that is if they can plan that far ahead. Stewey Langstrom and that crowd'll be stoned in a few minutes, if not already."

We both laughed, and then her face turned serious. "What about Shane, though. I wonder about him. Does he have plans for the future? Does he think about getting away from here and his … dad?"

We were in a line of moving traffic, heading out Campus Drive onto the main road that would take us into town and

Kristina's house. I thought about her question, unable to offer a quick answer.

She turned the volume down. "I mean it's okay if he doesn't. It's just that since I've got to know him—well, not really. Since I've been *trying* to get to know him, I can't help but think about his potential. I see him differently now, and I do think about him, probably more than I should."

"I've been trying to talk to him about it," I said. "His future I mean. But he doesn't respond much. It's hard to imagine Shane ever breaking away from his dad, but sometimes he gets this look, when I mention leaving for Auburn? A faraway look, like he's seeing something I haven't imagined. I never did get him to apply to any colleges. He always says, 'I'll think about it,' or 'maybe later.'"

"But he is smart, though. I know—"

"Yes, he's plenty smart. He could do anything."

"But will he? I mean without our help, without somebody to encourage and guide—"

"I don't know. I've been worrying about him for years, but what it all boils down to is Shane. He's gonna have to make his own future. Can't nobody do it for him." After those words came out I realized I'd answered more harshly than I'd meant to.

Kristina reached to turn the music back up. "Yeah, I guess you're right," she said. I tried to think of something to say, but I was afraid if I opened my mouth a squawk would come out. An unseen hand had turned my tone control toward bitchy, and for now the knob seemed broken. I didn't admit this to myself then, but Kristina's interest in Shane had begun to irritate, like sand in a bikini.

I liked the idea at first of them getting together. I thought it would be good for Shane, that Kristina could bring him out of himself and help him build confidence and social skills. But the thought of them *actually* being together as boyfriend and girlfriend, when I allowed it into my imagination, was like oxygen blowing over a bed of ashed-over embers. Emotions I didn't know I had— that shouldn't have been there—began to glow and spark, heating me up on the inside. I loved Shane, had been his defender, protector, guardian, friend, and—God help me—lover for years. I wouldn't admit it to myself, but I couldn't bear the thought of another, even my other best friend, stepping into any of those roles. Shane was mine, and a part of me clung to his—our—sickness in a way that could only compound our problems.

I suppose I could blame it on the barn, not the actual structure, but the mysterious power that resided inside, the force that tugged at me every time I passed by and that sometimes captured me when I was asleep, pulling me into a world where there were no parents or rules, a world of forbidden knowledge and experience. The dreams became stronger after Ernie's death and grew more complex as time passed. They never made sense but were rich and pleasant in texture, like French toast topped with maple syrup.

These subconscious adventures became part of who I was becoming in my early adolescence. I discovered my sensuality through these dreams and through them I became a girl. The barn contained not cows but horses, tigers, and other powerful animals, along with snakes and rats. The rats created a background noise of scurrying and twittering through hay. The snakes coiled around the support posts and beams, turning them into speckled, patterned barber poles through their sinuous movement. Shane was often there with me and sometimes other boys from school, and we always had the ability to fly. We could leap from our houses and soar through the stars into the barn's open loft door without leaving the twinkling night sky that was still visible above us through the cracks in the roof. Inside was an elaborate network of joists and rafters, under which lay an expanse of soft hay and beautiful antique furniture. Through gaps in the floor we could see the animals below, hear their pawing, chewing sounds and sometimes feel their breath. We weren't afraid of the animals, but they were there, and we didn't want to fall through the loft floor and land in their midst.

The loft, fractured and rickety, went on forever. There were beds and blankets and candles—we were always careful with those, being sure to blow them out. The barn always protected herself, whispering to us what to do. Another recurring feature was our near-nakedness. Shane and I were often in only our underwear. The other boys—I don't remember any girls—would be dressed. It didn't seem to matter to them that we weren't, but I always tried to cover my breasts with my hands. Sometimes Shane and I danced, and we did other things. Those episodes were always fuzzy after I awoke. I can't call them up now, but I do remember the feelings of shame that resulted from waking up wet between my legs.

Dreams this powerful predict and shape our realities. Soon Shane and I actually went inside, beginning a pattern that would be often repeated. The first time happened when we were thirteen, on the day after Christmas. Looking back, it seems that everything led up to that day.

∿

THE WHOLE BUNCH OF US had gotten together on Christmas Eve, a day that traditionally meant dinner and presents at MawMaw's. She always prepared the holiday ham, turkey and dressing meal with various side dishes and her wonderful desserts for us and the extended clan—a half-dozen of my great aunts, uncles, and cousins. The men would eat, smoke, and tell stories. The women stayed busy with serving and washing dishes. And the kids, when we were little, played underfoot, aggravating the adults and making too much noise in the house until the grownups got enough and drove us outside, except on bitter-cold or rainy days.

That year, the time together was awkward for us. We were getting older and we saw each other so seldom. A year was a long time and brought much change. From one Christmas to the next, we became different people. The adults, though, seemed to stay the same.

My great uncle Paul was a big shot with the power company. His youngest son Tyler, a football star, was a senior in high school that year. Everyone was talking about all of his scholarship offers and what a tough time he'd had deciding on the University of West Alabama over in Livingston. I had never heard of that school, but they all described it like it was the greatest place on earth. This attention distinguished Tyler from the younger kids and earned him a place at the grown-up table in the dining room while the rest of us—me, Shane, and three snotty cousins ranging in age from eight to eleven—sat around the dinette table in the kitchen corner.

I asked the youngest cousin, Greta, a pudgy girl dressed in a loose pink knit pullover, fashion jeans, and new sneakers with flashing lights in the soles, what she was hoping Santa would bring. She rolled her eyes. "I'm like eight years old," she said. "I know that Santa is really my parents."

"Well, still," I said. "Whoever Santa is, what would you like to see under the tree in the morning?"

"New clothes and bracelets, and new accessories for all of my Barbies, and an iPod."

"An iPod, those are great! Which one are you getting, Nano or Shuffle?"

"I've already got a Nano. I'm getting the one that just came out, with a touch screen. I want an iPhone, but Mom says I'm too young."

Her mom, a stylish young woman named Gerri, worked as a buyer for the Macy's store in Atlanta. Greta turned back to her plate and proceeded to stuff her cheeks with MawMaw's pecan pie. I realized she must have been bored with being there, that she and her family came to MawMaw's house out of a sense of obligation or curiosity. Suddenly, those of our kin who had moved away from Tanner County became total strangers in my mind, like people in the movies. I imagined they thought of us as folks to pity or to look at once a year as a reminder of how fortunate and talented they were to have found a different kind of life in the cities, where important people did important things.

The two other kids at the table were brothers, ten and eleven, who were always in their own little world. They had brought with them elaborate robot toys capable of sensing their environment and carrying out all sorts of commands. These things were about two feet tall, and they had taken over the table top with their dancing, high fives, and kung-fu moves. They even talked at high volume. One kept saying, "Who's your daddy?" The other one repeated, "I've cleared the area. It's safe to proceed." For a few minutes I was fascinated with them, but I could tell they were getting on Shane's nerves. He finally responded when one of them almost toppled over into his plate. He snatched the thing up by its flexible plastic waist and thrust it into its owner's face. "You need to get this thing away from me before I break it in half."

The kid froze for a moment as his robot made futile walking motions while being held off the table top. The seriousness of the situation sank in, and he reached for his toy after pressing something on the controller to make it stop moving. He and his brother turned away from us then to huddle with their robots in the corner. I looked at the scowl on Shane's face and said, "Let's go outside."

The day was gray, warm, and damp. I preferred blue skies and sun during winter, even if they brought colder temperatures. Drizzly, foggy days on end made everything seem stale and moldy, even my imagination. We tried to have fun on these days, but the dampness stifled enthusiasm, and we were always getting fussed at for tracking mud inside. We couldn't stay cooped up, though, especially on this day.

Daddy had hinted earlier of a big Christmas surprise. He and Uncle Rayford both knew that Shane and I wanted an ATV, a four-wheeler. As we poked around outside, we couldn't resist looking for their hiding place, or at least evidence that our dream might come true.

There were still some leaves under the trees out back, along with the cracked and rotting remains of the pecans that MawMaw and PawPaw had not gathered. She had picked up enough to make a couple of pies, and PawPaw had raked the leaves a while back, but they weren't as energetic about these chores as they had once been. The lumpy ground of the garden spot behind the well house was still covered with withered stalks and vines. Each year my grandparents grew enough vegetables for all of us and most of the neighbors. Toward the end of each summer, PawPaw, about worn out, would complain and talk about cutting back on the planting next time or even doing away with the garden, but I knew when winter had passed and he got a whiff of those warm spring breezes, he'd be out there on his tractor, breaking up the soil and laying off rows. I had faith in my grandparents, and it was hard to think of them changing, growing older and weaker. But it was happening, their bodies moving closer to old age and infirmity each day, just as surely as mine was moving through puberty toward adulthood.

There wasn't much out there to do, besides throw dirt clods and pecans at each other, so we decided to snoop inside the sheds and barn. Everything was familiar, like PawPaw's overalls and the smell of his pipe tobacco when we were kids squirming on his lap, an atmosphere that felt comfortable and permanent but not the least bit exciting. Shane and I had reached the age of constant boredom, when the need for scary secret sensations outweighed our need for comfort and security. We sought out new adventures each day. That's why we were eager for a four-wheeler as our big Christmas surprise. The prospect of riding through the pastures and exploring trails and logging roads thrilled us. A four-wheeler for Shane and me represented freedom, adventure, and fun in grown-up measures and would mark the fact that we weren't kids anymore.

PawPaw's barn wasn't big enough to hide something that large, with a hallway in the middle where his tractor resided and two small stalls on each side that were used for storing junk—plastic buckets, glass jars, hubcaps from old cars, parts for the tractor, and a broken chair or two. The tiny loft, rickety and dirty, held nothing but scattered piles of loose hay so old it was turning to dust, a few warped unfinished boards in one corner, a short length of rusty pipe, and a cracked plastic raincoat.

The open sheds built off the outside walls of the barn contained lawn and garden tools, some old fence posts, and coils of rusty barbed wire. There was nothing new or different. We had been playing here for years and had explored every inch hundreds of times. On this Christmas Eve we could find nothing that suggested a preliminary visit from Santa.

"Well," I said, tossing a dirt clod at the old scarecrow that stood haggard and forgotten in last year's garden, "maybe they're going to a lot of trouble to surprise us. You know they wouldn't leave it anywhere we could find it."

"We shouldn't get our hopes up," Shane said. "Winter months are slow for Daddy. He ain't had much work lately. Four-wheelers are for rich kids anyway, not people like us."

"People like us? What do you mean? We're as good as anybody."

"Really? Like our cousins in there? We as good as them?"

"Yeah. We're better than them. They're stupid. And fat."

"And nerdy."

"Stupid, fat, nerds. I'm glad we only have to see 'em once a year."

Shane smiled. It felt good to make that happen, to see—if only for an instant—the glint in his eye that was there before his momma disappeared. I imagined the old Shane returning bit by bit with each smile I managed to provoke, and I've continued to believe that bringing him back was my unique responsibility. Unfortunately, I haven't always gone about it the right way. I've learned that there's a price to pay for pleasing people and that sometimes what we think of as pleasure is really pain waiting to happen.

We hung around the backyard, barn, and garden spot with increasing boredom until it was finally time to go, and we were convinced there was no four-wheeler on the premises.

That evening and all through the next day I tried not to think about the disappointment that was sure to come. I tried not to think about how much my cousins and friends had. I tried to count my blessings. On Christmas day, like all the others I could remember, Mom, Dad, and I opened presents, laughed, played, and then sat down to a big breakfast. Only the expected items materialized that morning, so I quit thinking about anything larger than what I got: new jeans, sweater, Nikes, and an off-brand MP3 player. I was glad to enjoy that time with only my parents, but I wondered about Shane and Uncle Ray. I hoped the day wouldn't be too sad for them in that house, Rayford without a wife and Shane without a momma. I hoped they too would open presents and enjoy a big breakfast and that Rayford would ease up on the chores.

Christmas day passed, and on the day after I tried to act happy, at home with Mom and Dad. As we were finishing a light breakfast, Dad announced that later we were going to MawMaw and PawPaw's for a second Christmas dinner involving only our immediate families, the people I loved most. "Your MawMaw's still got lots of leftovers, and I still got plenty of appetite. We'll spend the afternoon over there enjoying good food and each other's company." I didn't want to go back to MawMaw's, having had enough of family and food for a while, but when Dad added that Santa may have left one more gift over there, I perked up.

"I got a feeling," he said, "that we may find another present, a special delivery, something Santa didn't have room for in his sleigh."

As Mom, still in her housecoat, gathered up the cereal bowls, she winked at me. Dad looked at my face for a response. The excitement, after accepting disappointment, was overwhelming. "Let's go now!"

"Just calm down," he said. "We've got to discuss some things—responsibilities, I mean."

"Sure, Dad. I'll always be careful when I ride."

"Well, it's more than a matter of being careful. You've got to care for her as well. You remember Ollie, your hamster? You did a good job of taking care of that little rodent. That's what convinced me you'd also do a fine job with this big girl. Same kinds of chores, really, just on a larger scale. Much more feed and water and clean shavings."

I was incredulous. I gazed into Dad's face for some sign that he was joking. "What do you mean, Dad? I wasn't expecting an animal—horse or whatever you're talking about—"

"No need to act surprised, Colleen. I've known how much you wanted a pony for years. And I noticed you and Shane poking around the barn looking for signs of one. Your dream has finally come true! Me and Rayford used his truck and a borrowed trailer to bring her over late last night. She's a pretty thing, sleek and ready to ride, a Welsh pony—small horse, really."

How could I respond? I thought Dad might be trying to trick me in order to produce a big surprise later, but I wasn't sure. What if he had really gotten me a pony and was anticipating my joyous response? I had wanted one for years, but that was when I was a little girl. I used to imagine having a close equine friend I could brush, feed, and care for, who would love me back and take me for leisurely rides through enchanted forests. But at thirteen I had given up those fantasies. I imagined instead rides and adventures that were more *unbridled*. The idea of a powerful motor revving beneath me that I could control with the slightest touch thrilled me, and I was especially excited about sharing these experiences with Shane. I knew he liked tinkering with mechanical things, and he was always talking about trucks, motorcycles, hotrods, and four-wheelers. Having one together would be fun for both of us and would help me to help him be happy.

As Dad stared at me, grinning, waiting for my response, I had trouble controlling my face. Finally, I decided to call his bluff. "I don't believe y'all got a pony. I think you're trying to trick me."

He smiled and spoke slowly. "It's okay, sweetie. Dreams do come true, and good things happen to good people. I'm just sorry you had to wait so long."

"Okay. Whatever. I guess we'll see in a little while. I'm going to start getting ready. You can let me know when it's time to go."

I needed to get away from Dad's grinning face and Mom's counter-top wiping and dish washing to my own personal space. I tried to console myself with the knowledge that Dad was a trickster. On Christmas and birthdays he would often try to fool me into thinking I was getting a lesser gift in order to heighten the effect of the present they had really gotten me, usually what I wanted or at least an off-brand version, like the MP3 player that was functional but not an iPod. I never expected first-rate, brand new, or top-of-the-line, but this Christmas I did expect a four-wheeler, at least a good used one, because Dad and Uncle Ray had led me and Shane in that direction weeks before.

But it had been a while since the four-wheeler seed had been planted, and no hints had been made recently to nourish the growing desire. I remembered saying something in early December to Daddy about how, when we got a four-wheeler, he and I could ride over to the old pond with fishing poles on a warm day, and he changed the subject, asked me if I was keeping my grades up and if I was ready for semester tests. I ended up not doing so great on my tests that year, but he didn't know that yet. It dawned on me that there were lots of things Dad didn't know about me, most importantly, that I wasn't a little girl anymore.

Then I felt silly sitting there in my room, which was still the room of a child. I didn't fit anymore with the pink and purple curtains and throw pillows, the stuffed animals, the cheap bookshelf filled with *Goosebumps* books. In one corner there still sat the pink plastic play kitchen I had since I was about five. It was stacked with schoolbooks and old CD cases now, but the fact that it was still there underneath the clutter prompted me to get up. I decided to confront Daddy about this pony thing, to remind him that I was growing and changing.

He was in the den, kicked back in his recliner watching a sports show with former athletes in suits talking about the upcoming bowl games. He barely looked up when I entered. "Dad," I said. "I need to talk to you."

He reached for the remote with slight annoyance and turned down the volume. "Okay. Shoot."

I sat across from him on our sagging loveseat. "About this pony … I mean, is that what you really got me? Because if it is, well … it's like this: I was kinda hoping for something else. I did want a pony, but that was before, when I was a kid. Now, I don't. I was thinking maybe you could take it back." Getting those words out was difficult, but I was glad I'd said them, at least at the moment. Saying them made me feel big for a few seconds.

Daddy looked at me, his face blank. Then he took the chewed-up toothpick out of his mouth and reached into his shirt pocket for a cigarette. His ashtray and lighter were on the end table. He lit his cigarette slowly and took a big drag. Words eased out of his mouth with the smoke. "I don't know what's got into you, little girl, but it seems you done got too big for your britches. You know that when I make a deal with a man, it's a done thing, so I expect you'll show some respect and appreciation for whatever you get. And I expect you'll take care of her like you're supposed to, and I also expect you to enjoy your gift of what you've always wanted. You'll bond with her, and a Welsh pony, by the way, is the perfect gift for a girl your age. I'm sure lots of people would be envious. So you just count your blessings and be happy, and that's all I wanna hear about it." He reached for the remote and turned back to his sports show.

I sat there dumfounded for a few seconds before returning to my little girl's room. My bed was there waiting. I pulled back the comforter with its pink, purple, yellow, and green psychedelic flower explosion and slithered in between the sheets, burying my face in the soft pink pillow. I didn't move until I heard Dad outside my door yelling, "You about ready? Time to go to your MawMaw's."

The short ride over was awkward, made worse by the feeling of being awakened just when I was beginning to doze off. We all seemed grouchy, tired of Christmas and each other. I perked up a little at the sight of Uncle Ray's truck when we turned into the driveway of the old farm house. With Shane there I wouldn't have to endure the impending disappointment alone.

I expected to see him in the yard, maybe even clomping around on the pony, but as Dad parked, all I saw was the dreary gray space occupied by the barn, sheds, and pecan trees. I looked for him to come out onto the back steps as we were getting out of the pickup, but he didn't. It wasn't like him to sit in the house, especially after I'd arrived. I stood there, puzzled. When I focused my attention on the barn, it looked just as it had the last time I'd seen it. There was no evidence of fresh hay or shavings or anything to indicate the presence of a large animal. I looked at Dad. He lifted his eyebrows and shrugged. Mom winked. Then I heard it, from a distance beyond PawPaw's fences the sound of a small engine revving, purring and snarling, getting closer. When I looked at Dad, I noticed a smile beginning to form.

He motioned with his head toward the barn. "Well, don't just stand there. Why don't you go and see your new horse."

My emotions were tripping over each other. "Dad, I can see from here there's no horse in there. You're still trying to trick me and, and … what's that sound? I hear a motor out in the pasture." My voice and my body were both bouncing up and down.

I looked from Dad to Mom. She was grinning, trying to keep from laughing out loud. She turned away shaking her head.

"I don't know," Dad said, "but it sounds like it's getting closer."

I ran toward the motor sound at an angle adjacent to the barn, toward the broken-down barbed wire fence and the overgrown field that had once been PawPaw's pasture. In the distance, beyond the brown weeds and stalks, stood an expanse of hardwood trees, and I knew there were some old trails and logging roads in there. The terrain sloped so that I could only see the tops of the trees, but the sound was coming from those woods and getting closer.

I formed a vision of what I hoped I'd see. Walking back and forth along the fence line, I tried to control my anxiety over its not appearing sooner. Glancing back I saw Mom and Dad still standing by the pickup watching me. Their smiles confirmed that this was working out the way they'd planned.

The engine sound slowed, then picked back up, revving through gear changes. During the lulls, I heard voices I couldn't make out. Finally, after not hearing anything for long moments, I heard the engine revving again—coming closer, coming fast!

When they broke into view on the dirt road, my pent-up emotions overflowed, fluttering down my spine to my feet. I ran toward them as they slid into the driveway, Shane driving, Rayford sitting behind. They were both grinning and Shane's hair was windblown. He looked at me as he turned the key to kill the engine. The throaty burbling stopped but Shane's smile remained. It was beautiful, and I was happier at that moment than I'd been in a long time, happier than I've been since.

We all stood around the four-wheeler admiringly, talking, laughing, and pointing out details. On the plastic gas tank a decal proclaimed, "Kawasaki," then in smaller letters "Bayou 220." The back fenders sported matching skull decals with black eye sockets and flames for hair. There were more decals and stickers on the sides and front fenders, and I noticed some dings and scratches. Overall, the machine seemed rugged, ready for adventures, and I trembled to think that I'd soon be riding a powerful, adult-sized ATV.

Rayford said, "She runs great, and Shane's done mastered shifting the gears. He can teach you, Collie. Ain't nothing to it."

Dad noticed me eying the skull decals. "We can probably get them off," he said. "The fella we got it from put all that on there."

"It's okay," I said, "looks great—I like it!"

Shane turned to his daddy. "Can we go ride some now? Me and Collie?"

"I don't see why not."

Momma said, "What about dinner? We're gonna be eating in a little while."

"It's early yet," Daddy said. "They can eat when they get back. We got all afternoon. Let 'em enjoy this warm weather."

"Well, still—I'll worry if they're gone too long. And what about helmets? You said you were gonna get helmets."

"We'll have to get them later. They're kinda pricey."

Momma scowled and Daddy added, "They'll be fine. It ain't like they're gonna be racing or doing stunts, just riding slow on easy trails. Safe as a pony, or bicycle."

Momma knew she was outnumbered. She hugged me and said in my ear as I was settling myself onto the seat behind Shane, "You be extra careful, Sweetpea. I love you." Then she hugged Shane, pressed her cheek against his, and told him to be careful.

Shane pressed a button on the handlebars and the engine came to life. The men were grinning and Mom was standing with her arms crossed over her chest as Shane gunned it and we spun out the driveway. I grabbed him around his waist and held on tight.

〜

GOING TO THE ROUND BARN wasn't even on my mind that first day we rode, but we somehow ended up there. The trails, I knew, wound around in that direction, but I had no idea they'd take us right up to the back side of the weather-beaten structure. We sat there at the broken-down gate for a moment before Shane switched off the engine. We'd never seen the barn before from this angle or from so close.

"Wow," I said.

Shane said, "This place looks creepy."

He was right. I tried to hop off, but sitting in back made throwing my leg over him awkward. I poked him in the ribs to make him move. "Come on. Let's go look!"

I had to wrestle the sagging gate free from the briars and weeds. Soon I was standing in the overgrown lot looking up at the barn's looming features. I turned my head expecting to find Shane, but he was lagging beside the four-wheeler.

"Come on," I said.

"I dunno. I don't think we should go in there." He was looking at the faded "Posted—No Trespassing" sign tacked to the gatepost.

"Come on. Don't be a baby." Saying those words brought a twinge when I realized he was, in a sense, still a baby, developmentally stuck. I walked back and took his hand. "Come on, it'll be fun. We'll be like explorers."

Inside the barn was exactly as I'd imagined, but being there produced an unfamiliar feeling. Even though it had been unused for years, the smell was still there, a moldy animal smell that was inviting and repulsive at the same time. When we got inside the main hallway, I started shivering, but not from cold. This was a new kind of shiver that started at my tailbone, then moved up my spine and through my limbs.

Shane noticed and put his arm around my shoulders. "You okay? You cold?"

"A little."

"Maybe we should go. Maybe we've seen enough."

My voice trembled. "We ain't seen nothing yet."

Sifting through the visual array, my eyes adjusted slowly to the dusky interior space. The shivering subsided when I noticed a familiar shape in one of the stalls spaced around the perimeter. "Look. Is that what I think it is?"

We stumbled through the shadows to where a wedge of light shone through cracks in the wall on an old pie safe, a narrow upright cabinet with punched tin doors. "Wow. It's just like the one in MawMaw's kitchen."

Shane said, "Yep."

The thing was covered with grime and dust. I opened one of the doors, and it nearly came off in my hand. I shut it back as best I could. "Looks like it's about had it."

"Yeah, like everything else in here."

Then Shane saw something that caught his attention. "Look," he said, pointing to the hulk of an ancient pickup truck resting on flat tires at the far end of the hallway. He lost what little interest he had in the broken pie safe and ran off to get a better look. When I caught up with him, he was sitting behind the wheel, working it back and forth and pressing the pedals. "Awesome," he said, coaxing the gear lever through its positions. "This thing's in pretty good shape."

I stood there smiling at his excitement as he pushed, pulled, and turned the various knobs on the old metal dashboard. He had become like a kid at Christmas, completely absorbed in discovering a gift bigger than his expectations. Inside the shadowy, decaying world of the old round barn, the darkness lifted from his face, and that made me happy.

"Come on," he said, "get in. We'll go for a ride."

I laughed and ran around to the other side, pressed the metal handle, and pulled open the squeaky door. The truck was dirty but I didn't care. I climbed in beside Shane and laughed as he steered, shifted, and made motor sounds with his mouth. He was already a good-sized boy, so he was able to reach the pedals okay. He was acting like a kid, but there in the shadows, he looked almost like a man, like he was really driving. He reminded me of his daddy.

"You're right," I said. "This old thing is in good shape. I bet you and Uncle Ray could fix it up. Y'all can fix about anything."

The look of childlike wonder on his face slowly gave way to his usual blank expression, and he stopped steering. I didn't know what I'd done to produce this change, but

I wanted his smile to return. I wanted him to release whatever it was that made him silent and sad.

After a long moment he said, "Naa. Motor's probably froze up. And Daddy's always too busy. It'll probably just stay here forever, rotting away."

We sat silently in the truck, on that day after Christmas, for a few more awkward moments. Shane stopped pressing the pedals, put his hands in his lap. He said finally, "Can we go now? They didn't want us to be gone too long."

I felt like the barn's magic could bring back the lighter mood. "It's okay, we got plenty of time. And we ain't seen the loft yet."

"I dunno."

I pushed my squeaky door open and went to his side. "Come on," I said, pulling the handle. "There's no telling what treasure we'll find up there."

With a sigh, he stepped down and followed me across the center hall to the ladder-like stairs. He stayed right behind me as I went up. "Be careful," he said. "The steps might be rotten."

I tested each one with light pressure before I put my full weight down. "They're fine."

With no railing to hold to, the last few awkward steps required us to bend over and crawl up onto the loft floor. Our movement stirred up dust from the old hay, and I suffered a minor sneezing fit as I stepped out of the way to make room on the landing for Shane. He said, "Be careful." Loose hay covered the floor, so each step was uncertain. I hoped the boards hadn't rotted from rain coming through the gaps in the roof. The pain of falling through a weak spot—broken bones, blood—presented itself in my mind, but I shook it loose and took a few shuffling steps toward the far wall.

I paused when I realized how much better I could see. The sky had cleared. Cracks in the roof and an open loft door on the far wall let the afternoon sun shine in. The middle portion of the roof was losing its grip on the silo in the center. The gaps, acting as skylights, projected jagged shapes onto the floor. Beams of light, filled with floating dust, encircled me as I surveyed our surroundings. That moment—the old barn, the loft, me and Shane, even the dust in the air—solidified, became permanent in a way I still don't understand. Standing there I sensed, for the first time, that we were riding rippling waves toward eternity and that every moment somehow lasted forever.

I began to tremble again. Shane pressed against my side. "What's the matter?" he asked.

"I dunno. This place …it's all—so beautiful."

He didn't answer, just stared at me with a puzzled expression. I noticed a cluster of shapes along the wall nearest us, a shaded area under an intact portion of roof. "Look," I said. "Let's go see what's over there."

The floor felt sturdy underfoot and I moved over it with more confidence toward what appeared to be stacks of wooden crates, trunks, and an assortment of furniture. Shane stayed close behind, and soon we were rummaging through a pile of stuff that hadn't been touched in years.

First the crates. The one on top held little of interest—manila envelopes filled with cancelled checks, bank statements and old receipts going back to the sixties. We shoved it aside and dug into the next crate. Another envelope held older receipts, dating back to the forties. Deeper still to a heavy wooden box with rusty hinges and cracked leather handles. The lid was secured with a tiny brass lock. "Shoot," I said. "There's probably old jewelry and gold coins in here. We've got to open it."

Shane said, "Let's see." He pulled out his Case pocket knife and began to work it underneath the hasp, but he stopped before he made much progress. "I dunno, Collie. This don't seem right."

"Maybe not, but it's too late now. Besides, this stuff's been sitting up here for years. Nobody wants it, so it wouldn't be stealing, I mean if we did find something valuable."

He shook his head and went back to work. As soon as he got a grip with the blade and pried a little against the hasp, the screws pulled right out of the old wood. He looked at me as he put his knife back in his pocket. "Well, there you go."

The smell—mold, rust, and vanilla—reached me as I lifted the lid. The contents seemed similar to the other boxes at first, but deeper digging brought up a stack of faded black and white photographs. "Hey look!" I said, "Some old pictures."

Shane was rummaging through the contents of a dust-covered chifforobe standing against the wall. "Yeah, who cares. You should see what's in here. This stuff's not even messed up."

Dropping the pictures back into the box, I turned to see what he'd found. He had pulled open the door of the cabinet, and as I approached a faint odor of mothballs reached me. A man's dark gray suit, double-breasted with pinstripes, wide lapels, and big flaps over the pockets was hanging in there. Beside the suit were a couple of pleated dresses with shoulder pads, and long sleeves, like something an old fat lady would wear to church thirty years ago.

Shane pulled the suit coat off the hanger and put it on. It actually wasn't a bad fit, just a tad large. "Great," I said. "Now you look like a homeless person."

As he gazed at himself in the mirror on the inside of the cabinet door, I opened the top drawer and was surprised to find a neatly folded patchwork quilt. When I pulled it out and held it up, allowing it to unfold, a faint mothball fragrance escaped and brushed past me like a sprite. The quilt was soft and clean. It had rested safely inside the chifforobe, protected from dust, bugs, and weather, for no telling how long. Shane turned from admiring his new look to see what I had found. He said, "Wow."

"I know, right? Let's spread this out so we can get a good look at it."

He glanced around, puzzled for a moment as I held the quilt up off the floor. "Hold on a second." Still wearing the coat, he found some nearby hay bales and dragged them over, arranging them lengthways side-by-side, stacking four then placing two in front to make a sofa shape.

I chuckled at his ingenuity. "Perfect!" The quilt draped over the bales made a comfortable place to sit while we examined the various treasures that surrounded us. I brought over the wooden box with the old pictures, and Shane, curious, sat beside me.

Most of the photos had names and dates on back. The faded ones were portraits of people with stern expressions sitting in parlor chairs, mostly couples in fancy turn-of-the-century clothes. Mixed in with the ancient portraits were many 3x5 prints with narrow borders. One of these, dated 1920, showed four children posed in front of the old Hudson farm house. We were amazed that it looked so new. In our lifetime it had existed in various states of decay and was presently all but collapsed. The children's names were listed on back in neat cursive: Ernest Hudson, b1910; Gertrude Hudson, b1911; Vernon Hudson, b1914; and Abigail Hudson, b1915. The girls wore pleated dresses and socks. The boys wore knickers. We laughed at their clothes. Shane said they "looked gay." I wondered briefly about the names. I had never heard of Ernest or Gertrude, but I remembered Daddy, when he'd told me stories about the barn, referring to the Hudsons as Mr. Vern and Miss Abby.

Shane said, "Lemme see that box. There's gotta be something better in there than boring old pictures." He reached over my lap and lifted it by the handles. When he did, the leather broke and the contents tumbled out all over me, our makeshift sofa, and the hay-covered floor.

I said, "Oh shit!"

Shane said, "Dammit!" Then we were both on our hands and knees in the hay, picking up broken bifocals, watches, lockets, bracelets, and key chains, hurrying to get everything back in the box, as if trying to avoid getting into trouble. We grabbed up bits of straw along with the unboxed relics. Shane said, "I'm sorry. I didn't mean to."

Then I realized that nobody cared, that this was our place now, our stuff. We weren't going to get into trouble. I touched his arm. "Hey. Wait a minute. Look at me." He lifted his gaze from the floor to my face. "It's okay," I said. "Nobody's been up here for years, and nobody's ever coming up here again, except us. There's nothing to worry about."

His face went blank. "Oh. Yeah, I guess you're right." Then he laughed, a short little chuckle. "We're crazy."

"Yeah," I said, "we are."

We gathered up the remaining trinkets and placed them back inside the box.

Shane said, "Check this out," as he picked up an old leather billfold. "Maybe there's money inside." The wallet was flattened and shaped by the hip of its former owner, its tooled leather darkened and cracked. He flipped it open and spread its contents on top of our sofa. No money and not much of anything else: faded business cards, slips of paper that could have been receipts, a color snapshot of an old woman, and a driver's license issued to Vernon Hudson. The expiration date was October, 1997. The mug shot was of an old man, tired, wrinkled, and unhappy. The fact that this had been carried by Mr. Hudson, probably right up to the time of his death, fascinated me. As Shane peeked into every compartment of the wallet, I examined the plastic card closely, establishing a bond with this man who had been dead for over ten years and existed now as a local legend in the memory of my father and countless others.

I picked up the picture of the woman. Her face looked tired and wrinkled also, amazingly similar to Mr. Hudson's. Funny, I thought, how old couples grow to resemble each other over the years. I guessed their children would have had long, straight noses and high cheekbones also. Then it hit me. The couple who had occupied the Hudson place for so long, Vern and Abby, weren't husband and wife but brother and sister! Weird. The faces lingered in my mind as we reassembled the billfold and placed it, along with the old photos, on top of the other stuff inside the heavy box. I closed the lid, letting the now useless hasp rest against the soft wood. Shane slid the box back to its former location. Then he spotted something against the wall that caught his attention. "Look, old magazines," he said.

"Cool! Let's check 'em out."

National Geographic magazines, dozens of them— familiar yellow borders around stunning cover shots. We flipped through several, pausing to take in the more interesting pictures and old advertisements. Shane giggled at a spread devoted to a remote tribal people who didn't wear clothes—distended breasts and abdomens, sagging bare butts, pierced and stretched lips and ears, naked children with painted bodies—done in glossy color. "Look," he said, thrusting the picture practically into my face. "How would you like to live with these people?"

"I guess it'd be okay. Running around naked would be normal if everybody did it."

"Don't sound normal to me." Shane continued to rifle through the stacks, looking for more naked pictures.

I was skimming through issues as well but stopped when I hit an article on sharks, loaded with pictures of massive jaws and teeth and sinuous bodies swimming through shimmering blue waters. As I read captions about great whites' amazing abilities to sense small amounts of blood from miles away and the tearing crushing power of their jaws, Shane exclaimed, "Holy shit!"

Underneath the *National Geographic* stack were larger format magazines, and he had lifted one into the light and flipped it open. I looked up to find him staring into the pages. I knew from his reverent attitude that he had found a girlie mag. "Let me see that," I said.

I pressed against Shane to see what had captured him. Sure enough, he was ogling nude shots of shapely young women in seductive poses. Turning pages, we saw breasts, thighs, stomachs, and bare backs, but crotches were coyly covered. The girls had long, flipped-up hair and bangs, big eyes, and pouty lips. In some of the pictures they were smoking cigarettes. In others they wore black stockings with garters and high heels. There were lots of magazines underneath with titles like *Escapade, Cavalier, Swank*, and *Topper*, and as we flipped through them, we were met with a wide variety of provocative pictures, everything from hippie girls wearing beads and flowers in their hair to girls removing slinky evening gowns as if they were about to have sex with James Bond.

These magazines were old, and the stuff in them was pretty tame compared to the hardcore material that's available now, but neither Shane nor I had access to the internet, so our exposure was limited. The magazines provided a glimpse into a mysterious, forbidden world. I could tell from Shane's response, the way he lingered over each breast, nipple, and thigh, that he had never seen girl parts before. My innocence, however, by this time was not completely intact.

Billy Thornhill had recently become my "boyfriend," or at least he thought he was, and we'd been messing around some. Opportunities were rare, but we'd managed a few groping sessions, the most notable of which had occurred that fall at a middle school football game. We'd found a spot underneath the bleachers where Billy proceeded to make me wet and tingly with his fingers inside my pants. He'd also stuck his tongue in my mouth and unzipped his pants. As we continued our French kissing, he placed my hand on his stiff penis, and I was shocked by what came next. As Billy stood there in the shadows, panting, his thing jerking and oozing, I wiped my hand on his jeans and ran back to our seats high in the bleachers, where I tried to act like nothing had happened. He joined me a minute or two later with a sheepish grin. He sat against me and squeezed my hand telling me I was awesome and that he loved me.

This was exciting, confusing, and disappointing. Billy's touch was clammy and there was something in his face I didn't like, a look of ownership, a look that said he'd love me as long as I continued to make him do what he'd just done. He had a big pimple on his chin, and when I turned away, I remembered how Shane's face looked whenever he saw me and Billy walking to class together or holding hands beside the lockers. Shane looked sadder at these moments than usual, although he tried not to show disappointment, to act as if what I did didn't matter. As these thoughts came to me in the loft, I realized how much I did matter, probably more than anything else in his life, and I sensed that this day would be important for both of us.

I was getting tired of squatting on the floor by the stacks. "Come over here," I said, picking up three or four of the magazines. "We'll be more comfortable." I led him back to our quilt-covered hay bales. I started trembling again—after all, it was December—but as we settled next to each other, I quit shaking. We looked at the pictures together. As he lingered over a spread featuring a pretty brunette with especially large and shapely boobs, I asked, "You've never seen real ones, have you?"

He shook his head. "No."

"Never kissed a girl, either. Have you?" Before he could answer, I whispered to him, "Let me show you how." I placed my hands behind his neck and pulled him to me. He pulled back a little at first, but as I sucked on his lips and tongue and pressed against him, his resistance melted. He caught on pretty fast, and soon he was kissing me back like he knew what he was doing, like he meant it.

It didn't take long for us both to get excited, the feeling that comes from doing what feels good even though you know it's wrong. Touching Shane in this new way felt like I was reaching the part of him that had been hidden for so long, the source of his pain. I wanted to bring it out, to help him release the secret that had made him so different. And I wanted him to know that I loved him, no matter what.

Even though it was too cool that day for us to completely undress, Shane got to see and touch real girl parts for the first time, and before we left, my hands caused him to do what I'd made Billy do. We got fussed at back at MawMaw's for being gone so long. They said they were getting ready to come looking for us. We didn't make up much of an excuse, just that we were having so much fun riding we lost track of time. Soon everything was smoothed over and our family supper was especially enjoyable with Shane eating and smiling more than usual. We didn't mention the old barn.

We went back there regularly in the weeks and months that followed. The prediction Shane made on that first day about the ancient truck in the hallway proved correct. No one ever pulled that relic out of there. As far as I know the barn collapsed over it, and it sits to this day, rusting, covered with rotting boards, timbers, and slats. As far as I know, me and Shane were the only humans to go inside the barn during its final days as a standing structure. After that first day of exploring, we became familiar with the place, its hidden recesses, its dangers and comforts. As we repeated our visits, the old round barn became not just our secret, but a container of secrets, holding the unfolding mystery of ourselves within its decaying net of debris.

∼

CHRISTMASES CAME AND WENT, summers ripened and withered, but the essentials of our lives didn't change. We continued going to school and keeping secrets, and I continued worrying about Shane's ability to find his place in the world, how he would make it on his own. Even now, after reaching this so-called milestone, a point in our lives that by definition embodies change, our basic facts remained. I had been accepted by Auburn University for the fall semester, less than three months away, but that reality was fuzzy in my mind. They had accepted me, but I had not accepted the idea of a new lifestyle actually replacing my current state, this world that was so frustrating and painful yet somehow comfortable.

Leaving Shane, MawMaw and PawPaw, and Mom and Dad would be like ripping chunks of myself away, but I wouldn't be leaving Kristina. She was also going to Auburn! We were planning to share a dorm room. We were going to experience fun, adventure, and new challenges. We were getting out of this hick place. But Shane, it seemed, wasn't going anywhere.

As Kristina drove us away from the graduation traffic and our last official high school activity, our mood turned somber. I remained preoccupied with thoughts of my cousin and the difficulties of our relationship. Kristina sensed my discomfort and offered encouragement: "I know you and Shane are really close and you worry about him, but he's gonna be okay. Your family's great, and we won't be that far away. We'll be coming home lots on weekends, and we got all summer to spend time with him and help him decide on a future. I'll make a bet with you. Before we leave in August, I'm gonna get him to loosen up, teach him how to have fun. I know I can, that is if you'll help me a little with arranging things, providing opportunities."

I saw a glint from sweeping headlights that reflected in Kristina's eyes and illuminated her perfect white teeth. Her smile lightened the mood. I smiled back. "Okay. I mean you're right of course. And we do have time. To enjoy our summer—beginning right now!"

"That's right, sister. We just graduated. We did it. Now it's time to party!"

She raised her hand in a high-five gesture and we slapped skin as she steered onto the main highway.

We hadn't gone far before both our phones got busy receiving text messages from friends. There was no definite plan for the night and the few details we had were shifting. Kristina handed me her phone, which was busier than mine, so she wouldn't be tempted to text and drive. I sorted and relayed the messages and replied, with her input, as best I could. Conner Evans's party was still on, but people couldn't decide when to get there or what to do first. Word was out that Stewey Langstrom was throwing an alternative party at his girlfriend's house because her parents were "cool." Griff Baxter, a big country boy who wore boots and camo to school everyday, was having a bonfire by the lake in his granddad's pasture. Most of Kristina's friends wanted to go to Olive Garden first, but there was disagreement on what time to meet. In the midst of all this my phone startled me with the unfamiliar ringtone that indicated an actual call rather than a text. It was Shane from their landline.

"Hello, cuz," I answered. "What's up?"

His voice sounded less hesitant than usual, almost excited. "Where are you?"

"I'm with Kristina. We just left the school. Headed to her house. Why? Is something wrong?"

"Everything's fine. I just wanted to know what was going on, and if I could still hang out with y'all."

"What? You mean you can leave? What about Uncle Ray and work?"

I got only silence for a second before Shane said, "He changed his mind. I told him Kristina invited me. He's liked her ever since that time she ate with us at MawMaw's."

"That's awesome!" I turned to Kristina. "Shane's dad's letting him out of the house after all. He changed his mind 'cause he likes you."

She leaned closer to me and shouted into my phone, "Yay Shane! Party time!"

I giggled and pushed against her shoulder. "You watch the road."

Shane asked, "Well, what? Do I meet you somewhere?"

"Rayford letting you use the truck?"

"Yeah, and he gave me some spending money. I can stay out late as I want and take the day off tomorrow."

This news was too mind boggling to consider at the moment. All I could say was "Wow."

I turned to Kristina. "Olive Garden?"

"Yep. That'll work. Tell him to meet us there in thirty minutes."

We stopped at Kristina's house to change clothes and freshen up. That took longer than we'd anticipated. We were nearly an hour getting to the restaurant. After we got on the road to Aaronville, I started worrying about Shane. It occurred to me that his restaurant experience was limited and he might not know what to do if he arrived before us. He didn't have a cell phone so I couldn't call.

The parking lot was crowded. We looped all the way around looking for a place. In the shadows of the back corner I spotted the rear end of the battered pickup. What a relief! As we got closer, I saw Shane's head through the back glass. He'd been sitting there waiting for us. Kristina finally found a parking spot, but before getting out of her car, we each had to check our faces. When I opened the door, I was startled to find Shane standing there. "Hey," he said.

It took me a second to recover. "Hi. What's up? Sorry we're late. Blame it on Kristina. It took her forever to get ready."

His eyes darted and he blinked before he spoke. "Y'all look … pretty."

Kristina replied before I could. "Thanks. You don't look too bad yourself, big guy." Then she smiled and winked. "Come on," pressing against him, "let's go inside."

Damn, she sure was cute. And Shane looked nice too. He had on a button-down plaid shirt, khaki slacks, and a pair of Sperry-style boat shoes I'd never seen him wear before.

The waiting area was packed with mostly teenagers. Some of our classmates were already there along with a bunch of kids from Aaronville High who had also just graduated. Kristina pressed through to the hostess station while the other kids giggled and messed with their cell phones. The harried hostess ignored Kristina at first until she said, "Excuse me. Excuse me, miss. We need to all be *together*." She made a circular motion with her arm. "All of us … Hey! County kids, y'all look this way." Then, smiling at the hostess, "This group. Looks like about twenty of us."

"Yes ma'am. We're putting some tables together now. Shouldn't be but a few more minutes."

Jennifer Muzik looked up from her cell phone. "Yeah, Kristina. Chill. I've got this taken care of." She held up the little square gadget that would blink and vibrate when our places were ready.

Kristina smiled. "Okay, cool. I should have known. I just wanted to be sure they knew how many of us." She tilted her head toward me and Shane. Jennifer smiled condescendingly at me without acknowledging my cousin except for allowing her eyes to quickly sweep over the length of his well-dressed body.

Conner Evans looked up, barely glanced at Shane and me, then smiled at Kristina.

I realized then what a potentially awkward situation this was. With standing room only in the waiting area, I felt like we were on display for those fortunate enough to be seated. Shane's discomfort was a radioactive glow. He stood there with nothing to occupy his big hands. He shifted toward me and the door as if he would escape, but I reached up, touched his shoulder, smiled. "This is gonna be great. You ain't never had spaghetti like this, and salad and breadsticks—all you can eat. We're gon' have fun tonight."

He managed a little smile, then I heard a giggle. When I looked at Jennifer, she looked down with a smirk, barely holding her laughter in check. She spoke in a low voice to Conner. I couldn't make out all she said, but I heard the word, "hick."

Kristina, for the moment, had forgotten about Shane. She was chatting animatedly with some of the other cheerleaders. About that time Jennifer's gadget went off.

"That's us, that's us!" she said, holding the blinking thing up for all to see.

"This way, please," said the hostess, carrying an armload of menus. We all followed her into what became our own little room. Tables were placed together and chairs were adjusted. Kristina, Shane, and I ended up on one side across from Kyle Lambert and Billy Thornhill. Jennifer and her group, thank goodness, were at the other end. Several tables along the walls were claimed by smaller groups and spillovers. All in all, a neat arrangement that gave me the sense that this could turn out okay.

The place felt comfortable. I guess it was the décor. I craned my neck to look at the archways, exposed beams, stucco and brickwork, wine racks everywhere, and green plants. I imagined living in a big house like that and filling it with guests every night. Of course, I'd have a staff of servants to do all the work while I greeted and smiled and conversed graciously. This fantasy was short-lived. Shane's awkward presence and clenched jaw brought me back to reality. I started talking to him, pointing out items on the menu that I thought he might like. Then Kristina got involved, laughing, poking him in the ribs, and offering to share appetizers with him. Shane had become the center of our female attention, and we managed to help him relax.

Our time at the restaurant passed by without major incident, nothing more disastrous than what you'd expect from a bunch of teenagers who'd just graduated. We stuffed ourselves, laughed, and made huge messes at our tables while the servers took our ridiculous demands in stride. We weren't out of control, except when it was time to go. That's when Conner, show-off that he was, did something that was over the line, a childish act that brought back my anxiety.

He thought it would be cute to pull that old trick of putting his tip, a five-dollar bill, under an overturned glass of water. Jennifer thought this was hilarious. "Conner Evans," she said through her laughter, "you are too *bad!*" Other kids laughed too. But not Shane. He didn't think it was funny.

"Why'd you do that," he said, standing.

Conner looked confused for a second. "What?" He turned to Jennifer. "What did he say?"

Shane answered, "I said, 'why'd you do that?'"

Conner collected himself. "Well—Shane, isn't it?—I did it because it's funny. You know, to get a laugh." His condescending smile was sickening, as if he were indulging a naughty third-grader.

Shane said, "Ain't funny to that waitress. She's been working hard trying to take care of us. It's a dirty trick."

"I see. Well, Shane, I don't want to get anybody upset. And it does look like someone is gonna have to clean up spilled water. Maybe extra compensation will make it right." He pulled out his billfold, extracted a ten, and placed it next to the overturned glass. "How's that, buddy?"

Shane glared at him without answering. Conner, with a flip of his head to settle his dark bangs in their prescribed place, said, "All right, then. I say it's time to party! Let's get outta here!"

Following his lead, we made our way out of the Olive Garden in our various groups and pairs and climbed into our vehicles. The pairings that formed, though, weren't exactly what I'd had in mind. Billy Thornhill conveniently asked Kristina if he could ride with us. She thought that was a great idea, so, after a moment of anxiety over who would sit where, I ended up in the back seat with him, fully aware of what he had in mind. Oh well, I thought, maybe I should give the guy another chance. And by giving him a chance, I'd be giving Shane a chance with Kristina. Billy wasn't so bad, really. He'd been more or less devoted to me since eighth grade, even though I rarely acknowledged him. A sad fact took flight inside my brain: my unhealthy attachment to my cousin had caused me to ignore boys who liked me. Maybe this was the beginning of positive change, a move toward normalcy. I tried to stay upbeat. Kristina was laughing, joking around with Shane about how he'd put Conner Evans in his place. Shane was smiling. Billy was excited over the opportunity to finally get close to me. I couldn't let my emotional discomfort bring the others down. I had to do my part to make this a special night, a night to remember.

Conner Evans's house was the fanciest one in an upscale development on the outskirts of town. His family had moved down here a few years back when his dad opened a Hyundai dealership out near the interstate. The whole family seemed to be immediately successful in Tanner County. Everybody loved them with their nice clothes and smooth Michigan accents. Lots of Ford and Chevy people bought Hyundais. Conner and his two younger sisters rose to the apex of popularity within their classes. Conner always drove a brand new car. He'd upgraded twice since sophomore year and was currently driving a pearl white Genesis coupe with black accents.

Conner being Conner, he had to show off as soon as he pulled out onto the main highway by squealing tires and leaving us in the rubber smoke. Kristina took this as a challenge. "Oh hell no!" she said. "You can't leave Kristina's coupe that easy." She gripped the wheel and straightened her right leg out against the floorboard. "He thinks he's hot shit in that new car. I'll show him. I'll run this little baby right up his ass."

Billy shouted over the whine of the engine, "Hell yeah, you go girl!"

Conner's taillights were pulling away, but Kristina, determined, kept her foot in it. Billy was laughing, rocking back and forth. From where I was I could watch the speedometer climb. We were up to about eighty when Shane said, "Whoa, girl. Why don't you ease off a little and let that fool go on. He ain't worth it. You ain't really gotta follow him do you? I mean, you know the way to his house?"

She cocked her head. "Sure. I been there a bunch of times … . You're right. He's not worth a speeding ticket."

The engine whine dropped an octave as she let up on the accelerator. I breathed a sigh of relief as the speedometer eased back down into the range of sane driving. With renewed faith that we may actually make this trip in one piece came another feeling, one of wonderment over Shane's newfound assertiveness. He had challenged Conner over his rudeness at the restaurant, and he had spoken to Kristina, in a voice of reason and authority, without being spoken to first.

Billy drove these thoughts away by opening his mouth and reminding me of why I'd been avoiding him all this time. "Damn, Shane, you ain't gotta be such a buzzkill, just when things are starting to get interesting. I believe we'd have gained some on him in the curves. Probably caught up with 'em by the time we got there."

"Hush, Billy," I said. "Shane's right. Conner Evans ain't worth it, not worth a speeding ticket or even the extra gas it'd take to go that fast. Let him show his ass. That's about all he's good for. Besides, in case you haven't heard, driving fast is dangerous."

"Don't you trust Kristina's driving?"

"Yeah," Kristina said, "Don't you trust me, after all we been through in this car?"

"I trust your driving as much as I trust anybody's. I just trust it more at a reasonable speed."

"Wow," Billy said. "That's awesome. Two buzzkills in the same car, and on our graduation night, even. Y'all need to loosen up, and I got just the thing to help with that."

He started rummaging in the backpack he'd set on the floor when he climbed in. "Here's my baby," he said, bringing up a bottle.

I said, "Yeah, right, Billy. I'm sure that's just what we need. What the hell is it, anyway?"

"Vodka, sweet thing. You 'bout ready for a taste?"

I gave him a look then turned away to gaze out the window.

"You ever tried it?"

"What, do I look like some kind of vodkaholic to you? No. I've never tried it."

"Didn't think so, but you really should tonight, Collie. This is a special night. A drink or two will help you have a good time, and it don't even taste bad. Mixes with almost anything. Check this out."

He set the bottle in the corner of the seat and reached into his backpack. "I've got one already fixed up for us. We can pass it around."

He brought up a mega-sized energy drink can with a resealable cap. "I know you've drunk this stuff before, right? Great with vodka." He unscrewed the top and took a big swig, then wiped his arm across his mouth. With a grin, he held the garish can out to me. "Here, try it."

∾

MY EXPERIENCE WITH BOOZE was limited, but I'd gained a healthy respect by observing Dad and his friends who would come over on weekends to drink beer and pick guitars. I could always tell when the alcohol was influencing their behavior. During those events, Roger, a short pot-bellied guy, was always first to cross the line. He was a few years older than Dad and usually wore a Crimson Tide cap to cover his balding head.

They'd set up under the big oak in the front yard, with several well-stocked coolers nearby, and I'd sit and listen until Daddy made me go inside. They were pretty good and could play a bunch of songs by people like The Marshall Tucker Band, Charlie Daniels, and Hank Jr., and at some point they'd always play "Sweet Home Alabama." One night last summer I had my chair pulled up right into their circle. It felt nice under the moonlit sky, stars visible through the oak leaves. The guys had placed citronella candles on poles and hung a big Coleman lantern from a low limb of the tree. Momma was in the house because she didn't approve of their drinking. When she called for me to come inside, Daddy said, "She's fine out here with us. Let the child enjoy some good music and conversation."

I was dressed as a typical teenage girl would be in the middle of summer: Nike running shorts in black with pink trim, and a pink half tee. I had on flip-flops and I'd just taken the pony tail out of my hair. I was enjoying the music and being part of something grown-up. I also enjoyed the attention I was getting from Dad's friends. They were all smiles and very nice to me.

The guys, as they finished off their beers, started asking me to grab them another so they wouldn't have to get up and set their guitars down. Their behavior was acceptable, and I felt that Daddy took some pride in me, knowing that I'd grown into a young woman whose looks and manner were appreciated by his friends. A pleasant bond formed between us as the men drank their beers and played their music. But this atmosphere changed abruptly when Roger got a little too frisky.

"Collie," he said, "grab me another cold one, sweetheart." The cooler was right beside where he was sitting, but he didn't want to get up. I told him no problem. As I bent over to reach into the wet iciness, I felt something touching my ass. Before I could step away the touch became a pat and I heard Roger say, "Umm, umm, what a sweet young thing." Then I heard the thrumping, banging sound of Daddy's guitar hitting the ground as he stood up.

"Whoa now," he said, "That's my little girl and ain't nobody gon' be touching her like that while I'm around." He balled his fists and moved across the circle toward Roger.

I said, "Daddy—" but before I could say more Roger started apologizing all over himself. His guitar slid off his lap as he raised his hands. "Naw, naw, Gene. I didn't mean nothing. It's just that she's so sweet, that's all, a sweet little thing and you're lucky to have such a beautiful daughter...." Everything froze as Roger kept blabbering about how sorry he was and how he respected me and daddy and would never do anything to damage our friendship and how much he wanted to make it right.

I found my voice: "Daddy, it's okay. He didn't mean no harm."

"Get in the house, Collie."

I knew I'd better do what he said, but before I could take two steps Daddy said, "No, wait. Roger, you are gonna make this right, dammit. You're gonna apologize to Collie, like you mean it. Tell her you respect her and from now on you'll treat her right, like she's somebody."

Roger blubbered on as I stood there for what seemed like forever, his speech slurred and his voice cracking. His eyes were moist in the lantern light. He said he knew I was a fine young lady and that he never had a little girl of his own and he'd been lonely for a long time and he just forgot himself and would I please, please forgive him? I felt shaky and sick and I'm sure the other guys were also uneasy. I didn't know what to say. Finally somebody started picking the opening notes of "Dueling Banjos" from that old move *Deliverance*. Another guy slowly picked out a response. The musical conversation continued and began to gain tempo.

I looked at Daddy. He shrugged and went back to his chair. I said, "I think I'll go in now. Momma might need some help in the kitchen." He nodded and winked. As I walked away, I gave in to a mischievous impulse. "Roger, you can get your own damn beers from now on." I heard laughter from behind me as I moved toward the safety of our house.

⮕

THERE'S A TRADITION at my school, a popularity contest, that honors a chosen group of seniors with "superlative" distinction in a variety of categories, such as Best Dressed, Most Intellectual, Most Likely to Succeed, Wittiest, and others. I'm sure this goes on in other places, but at my school it's a big deal. Competition develops over who gets chosen to which category, as some are more desirable than others. The top superlative spot, the very pinnacle of achievement, is Mr. and Miss TCHS. This title is awarded each year to the most popular, cutest couple. Our class voted to honor none other than Conner Evans and Jennifer Muzik with this distinction. I didn't vote for them but obviously a bunch of people did.

While the importance placed on this tradition turns my stomach, I'm proud that Kristina made the superlative list. She was voted "Most School Spirit," which is ironic considering she hates our school and has always been quick to point out that Tanner County is a place for losers. She doesn't hate the people, just the place—the smallness of it, the pointless rituals and narrow-minded attitudes. Being able to muster enthusiasm, as she did each Friday night in autumn under the lights and throughout the long winter basketball season in that smelly old gym, is a gift. I was there and I remember many times having to look to her for inspiration when I felt my spirit ebbing. Enthusiasm sometimes has to be faked, but at least Kristina was able to fake it from her heart—if that makes sense—because she wanted things to be better, not because she wanted attention or approval.

All the other superlatives, the entire cute, perky, witty, well-dressed, and talented bunch, ended up at Conner's party. Kristina fit right in, Shane and me, not so much. But thankfully, we weren't the only non-superlatives. Conner generously opened his home to the losers as well as the chosen ones, and the wannabes were well represented. The only thing I wanted to be was close to Shane and Kristina and for everything to work out okay for the people I loved.

The couple named "Most Talented" was in rare form by the time we arrived. We'd made a stop along the way at Buck's Hilltop Gas and Convenience so Billy could buy a couple more of those big energy drinks. He poured out about a third of each one then refilled them with vodka. One can he passed to Kristina for her and Shane; the other he kept for us. We each took several swigs on the way. We heard music and laughter as soon as we parked the car and started up the cobblestone walkway to the entrance of Conner's house.

Kristina pushed open the heavy oak door and we stepped into a marble-floored foyer with a vaulted ceiling. The center of attention was a grand piano and a couple playing and singing for the crowd. Brad Winsley was tickling the ivories like one of those great jazz players from back in the day, accompanying Britney Baker, who was scat singing, hitting a fantastic range of notes, trilling up and down the scale with wonderful musical nonsense. I knew Brad and Britney were voted most talented, but I didn't realize they could play and sing like that. They had everybody dancing and clapping, and their performance set a promising tone for the party.

As Brad and Britney reached the end of a number, Mr. Evans entered the room wearing khakis, boat shoes, and a polo shirt. He looked robust with a ruddy complexion, flat stomach, and dark hair graying at the temples like a commercial for men's hair color. He gestured to Brad to stop playing, and spoke in a genial but commanding voice: "Attention grads, attention everyone." He gazed around the exquisitely appointed foyer at the young smiling faces turned to his in anticipation. "First, let me say that I'm very proud of you. You did it! You've reached a milestone in your lives, and I'm proud—*honored*—to be a part of your celebration, here in my home. Our family welcomes you and I hope you'll have the time of your lives!

"This is indeed a celebration, not just of past accomplishments, but of what you will accomplish. I truly believe that this class, this room full of grads, will change the world. Maybe you guys will be able to straighten out the mess you inherited from my generation." He waited for a few chuckles to subside. "Now, I do need to go over a few—a very few—ground rules.

"Conner's mom and I will be going to bed way before you guys, so we've set up the basement as party central. Please understand that I'm not providing alcoholic beverages to you, but there is a large refrigerator and several tubs of ice downstairs stocked with beer and wine coolers. I'm not encouraging you to drink those. I am encouraging you, though, not to drink and drive. Please use a designated driver or feel free to spend the night. There's plenty of room—sleeping bags, extra beds, inflatable mattresses, futons, and such. Use your cell phones to let your parents know where you are. And you do not have my permission to drink the alcoholic beverages that are in the basement. I wouldn't encourage you to do anything your parents wouldn't approve of. If you look hard enough, you can probably find some soft drinks." Again his eyes panned across the room, and he smiled, nodded, and winked at his audience. This guy was smooth. I could see how he had become so successful.

Three houses the size of the one I lived in could fit inside the basement of the Evans home. The first place where a crowd started gathering was set up as a music room with drums, amplifiers, guitars, and a portable keyboard. I think the idea was for Brad and Britney to continue their performance and keep the positive energy going, but others wanted to get in on the act. Conner got behind his drum kit and tried to be cool with fancy cymbal stuff and twirling his sticks, but it sounded like he was playing a different song. His timing was way off. Then Dexter Gaddis plugged in an electric guitar and started hitting power cords in the wrong key. After a few minutes of this, I sought shelter from the racket. I got Kristina's attention and motioned with my head. I knew she'd understand my nonverbal message: Let's get out of here. I led the way, she pulled Shane along, and Billy followed us into the hallway.

There were people out there too, so we hung around talking to friends and taking a few more swigs from the monster drinks. The noise level was still too high, making me feel edgy. I looked at Shane. He was smiling, nodding his head, talking to Kristina, or listening rather, as she talked to him. She was holding the drink they were sharing, laughing and waving her arms about. For the moment they seemed okay.

Billy kept nudging me with offers of another drink. "Here, baby. Try to keep up now," he shouted over the noise as he took another swig. Everybody else was drinking too—beer, wine coolers, hard lemonade.

Those who tried to converse were practically yelling. Many were dancing, laughing. My mood bounced up and down like a hyperactive kid on a seesaw. Shane and Kristina—what was going to happen with them? Some of the scenarios my mind constructed contained smiles, laughter. Others didn't. Billy kept pressing against me, rubbing the small of my back, winking, smiling, and offering me the monster drink. The antics of my classmates were funny but also disturbing with the crude dancing and sexual innuendo. I'd never been around so many people in various stages of drunkenness. Each time my seesaw hit bottom, I found myself reaching for another drink.

I'd seen how booze could cause things to move unexpectedly from warm fuzziness to ugliness, even violence. Watching my classmates make fools of themselves made the hairs on the back of my neck stand up, but as I took more swigs from Billy's monster drink, I found myself not giving a shit. It was a weird feeling, keenly aware yet reckless. Part of me wanted something to happen, to force some kind of change or major event. I remember thinking that letting go was good, that I needed to loosen up, to purge myself of eighteen years of bottled-up anger, frustration, and fear. Cleansing myself this way, I rationalized, would make me a new, better person, ready to face the challenges of adulthood.

My mood and the party's flowed together. The quality of sounds coming from the music room continued to decline, pushing more of us into the hall and adjoining rooms. Swept along with the movement, I found myself inside another impressive space, the Evans's home theater. A bunch of kids were already there, and they'd pushed the furniture to the walls, making a good-sized dance floor. The big flat-screen was showing a Sugarland video, and the surround-sound was pumping out the tune with lots of bass. People were dancing, some two-stepping, others flailing about.

I laughed when I saw Santricia Dobbs and Jamal Harris, the only African-American kids there, dancing to country music. They were laughing too and soon became the center of attention. Santricia—everybody called her Treecie— was a great dancer. Some said she was the token black girl on the cheerleading squad, but she had earned her spot. Recognizing her passion and talent, Ms. Lambert relied on Treecie as our choreographer. Whenever we needed a new routine, Treecie was the one who figured it out, teaching us the moves and how to pop the right attitude. I knew, as did the other cheerleaders, that her real forte was hip-hop. Her skills were amazing, and I wondered if she and Jamal were drunk enough to show what they could do.

As the song ended, Treecie hopped up onto a coffee table and started clapping her hands. "Hey y'all, listen up," she said in her throaty voice. "Y'all be moving awright, but you need to let Treecie show you how to get some real house party shakin' goin' on up in here. Jamal—where'd my man go? There he is. Jamal, find us something, baby. Y'all give it up to Jamal. Let him have the damn remote!"

She was laughing, as were the rest of us. Jamal started clowning around with some ghetto moves. "You got it, baby. Whatever you want."

Somebody said, "Here you go, man," and tossed him the remote. It took Jamal a minute to find what he was looking for, but just before Treecie's spell over the crowd wore off, the room began to vibrate with booming bass sounds. The huge hi-rez screen came to life with the quivering, humping butt cheeks of dozens of sexy females in various stages of undress. The scene was filmed in an inner-city warehouse with brick walls, exposed beams and pipes. There was definitely something going on in there. Big black dudes in thuggish dress, gold chains and bracelets, massive medallions swinging, pants swagging. Lots of crotch grabbing and things happening at once with strange violent images that didn't belong, guys and girls blowing clouds of smoke. The biggest dude, Dr. Big Thump, was rapping over the chaos. As he sang, his face transformed into a series of grotesque masks, and the leading girl dancers backed up to him, simulating sex with their butts against his crotch. The camera panned to reveal in every corner, smoke, glitter, skin, and frenetic ass movement. The video reached a climax with Dr. Big Thump pointing around in a pronounced rhythmical fashion, commanding all to "Twerk it! Twerk it! Twerk it!"

Treecie, still on the table was showing how it was done. Other girls joined in, trying to duplicate the jiggling twerk moves with varying degrees of success. Of course, the guys loved it. They were clapping and cheering. In the midst of all this MawMaw's face popped into my head. She was saying, "Lord, I ain't never seen such," a statement which perfectly conveyed my own feelings. The spectacle going on around me was fascinating, but I couldn't shake that prickling at the base of my neck.

Shane. Where was he? How was he taking this? I scanned the room until I found him standing alone in the opposite corner. He had that look again, sorely out of place with his big hands hanging at his sides. Kristina had joined the other popular girls in the ass-shaking frenzy. She was in front of everyone, hamming it up with Treecie. There was a look of abandon on her face as she worked her petite booty, as if she'd never felt better in her life. Most of the guys were clapping and chanting, "Twerk it, twerk it, twerk it …." Shane looked pitiful.

Billy nudged me. He was grinning and shouting, but I couldn't make out what he was saying. He held out the can. I took it. He shouted again and gestured with his head. I understood then that he was saying I should be up there twerking with the rest of the cheerleaders, for his and the other guys' entertainment. I handed him back the can, and from out of nowhere pushed hard against his chest. "Fuck you," I said. Then I started making my way to the other side of the room where Shane was standing. I didn't look back, but when I reached my cousin, I was relieved to see that Billy hadn't bothered to follow me.

Shane's eyes told me he was glad I'd come to rescue him. He managed a little smile. "Come on," I said, motioning with my head. I took his calloused hand, and he followed me around the perimeter of the big room back into the hallway.

"Getting a little too crazy in there for me," I said.

He nodded. "Yeah. I ain't never seen such."

We stood there grinning at each other as our classmates, spillovers from the other rooms, mingled about us. A couple was making out, the girl pressed against the wall, one leg entwined around the guy's hip. Another couple ducked into a bedroom. At the end of the hallway I noticed a set of French doors, which gave me an urge to go outside for some air. As I reached for Shane's hand, I saw he was still holding his monster drink. He took a swig then offered it to me. "No thanks," I said. "I've had about enough of that stuff."

"Yeah, me too. Pretty good, though. You know, I've never been drunk before. You think I'm drunk now?"

I held him at arm's length to get a good look. He was swaying, and his lips and eyes were wetter than usual. He blinked languidly.

"No," I lied. "You seem fine. About like always. You feel okay?"

"I feel great. Better than ever. Collie, I think … I need … to tell you some stuff."

It's hard to describe what I felt at that moment. There was warmth inside of me, getting warmer, like water in a pot just before it boils. "It's okay. You know I love you. We'll have time to talk later. Now, though—" I made a sweeping motion with my arm— "here we are. This is a very important night. Let's make the most of it. Let's enjoy this party at our rich classmate's house. I mean, we're here so we belong here, right? We're as good as anybody, remember?"

He nodded. "Yeah. I remember. We're here. We made it, didn't we?"

"We made it, cuz. Come on, let's get some fresh air." I gave him a gentle tug and he followed me toward the French doors. But before we could go through, we met Conner Evans, coming out of the bathroom.

"Hi guys," he said. "Everything okay? Having fun?"

"Yeah," I answered. "Great. Just thought we'd get some air."

Conner smiled. "Things getting a little too crazy for you in the video room?"

"Were you there? I didn't see you?"

"Yes, in the quiet corner, observing. Actually, Jennifer and I were sitting beside Kristina and Shane here, before the twerkfest began. So, I'm just like you guys. I need some relief."

I glanced at Shane. He was nodding and smiling.

Conner smiled back. "Where's Billy what's-his-name? Weren't you with him earlier?"

"Yeah, sorta. He's still in there cheering on the dancers."

He laughed. "Those girls don't need much encouragement. Such show-offs. I think Jennifer and Kristina were in competition trying to keep up with Treecie."

I found myself smiling and nodding like Shane. I didn't know what to say.

"You, though, seem different. I don't see you as a typical cheerleader."

Conner paused to wait for my reply. When he realized there would be none he said, "Come on. We can hang on the patio, take a little break." As an afterthought he turned to Shane. "That sound like a good idea? We can relax and chat for a minute. I'm sure the twerkers will find us soon enough. The parties always end up out here anyway."

He pushed open the door and made a gesture for me and Shane to go first. We stepped outside into another beautiful space. The patio was paved with the same cobblestones as the walkway out front. Glass-topped tables with umbrellas over them were scattered about, along with soft-cushioned outdoor chairs and chaise lounges. Colored lights were strung overhead, and candles burned on bamboo sticks. Trees were growing out of pots. There was a bar on one side under a green awning that matched the color of the furniture. The patio surrounded a shimmering blue pool, on the opposite side of which rested a separate building with brick columns in front, more tables, and an outdoor fireplace. I was speechless. Shane's eyes were wide with wonder.

As we sat at one of the tables, I managed to say, "Wow. This is really nice."

Conner said, "Thanks. We enjoy it. My parents like to entertain. As you can see, there's a bar out here—speaking of which, seems you two could use a drink. Shane, what can I get for you, buddy?"

"I'm good," Shane answered, holding up the monster drink.

"Hmm, I see. You trying to stay awake or is there booze in there?"

"Vodka," I said. "Billy's idea."

Conner nodded. "Vodka it is. I'll be right back." He walked over to the bar, leaving Shane and me alone in our amazement.

I was having trouble controlling my grin, my emotions in general. I looked across the table, raised my eyebrows. Shane nodded and did the same. "See," I said. "I told you."

"Told me what?"

"We belong here. Can you believe how friendly Conner is being to us? He's much nicer when Jennifer's not around."

"Yeah, I can't believe he's fixing us drinks. Here, help me finish this one." He turned up the monster drink then handed it to me. I drained what was left and looked around for a place to put the empty can. Not finding one, I set it under the table.

Conner returned carrying three drinks in real glasses. "Here we are," he said. "Salty dogs, my favorite. Hope you like them."

"Sure," I said. "Great. Thanks."

Shane said, "Thanks."

There was a lull. Before it became uncomfortable, Conner and I both said "So …" at the same time. He smiled. "Go ahead."

"When you said just now that I don't seem like a typical cheerleader? You're right. I was always a softball girl before. I played for years, rec ball and the school teams, all the way through tenth grade, the year y'all moved here. That spring I tried out for cheerleader. Don't really know why, but now I love it. All the other girls … I mean, they're great."

Conner was looking at me with a knowing smile. "If they're so great, why aren't you in there dancing with them?"

I turned away, glanced at Shane, shrugged my shoulders. I could hear the thumping bass of the hip-hop music and laughter from inside.

"It's okay," Conner said. "I understand." Then he turned his attention toward Shane. "I want to thank you, my friend, for putting me in my place back at the restaurant, for pointing out to me I was being a jerk. I need that sometimes—to be reminded how to treat people, especially when I get around Jennifer and her friends. I need people like you who are more … umm" —he struggled for the right word—"*connected* to the real world, who've had different experiences and can offer perspective."

Shane nodded and grinned as Conner continued. "I mean you guys are what my dad calls 'the salt of the earth.' I don't know where we'd be without people like you."

His meaning and intent were puzzling, but I realized that Conner had politely called us rednecks. I shrugged it off, gave him the benefit of the doubt, and enjoyed the new sensation of sipping from a salted rim. Then came a sudden surge of noise from behind me as the French doors opened, spilling out sounds of debauchery and a voice I recognized immediately, Jennifer Muzik squealing, "There you are! You should come back in, baby. Everybody's having a blast."

She shimmied around to Conner's side, draped her arm around his neck, and bounced her hips against him. "What are you doing out here? Fix me a drink."

"We were just having a nice chat and enjoying some fresh air," Conner said, rising from his chair.

Jennifer eased into the vacated spot. "Not too much ice, baby." Then she looked at me. "Hi, Colleen. Why weren't you dancing with us? Look at me. I'm all hot and sweaty, but it was worth it." She made little fanning motions with her hand in front of her face. A strand of dark hair was stuck to her forehead but her makeup was still in place. "I thought Kristina was gonna hurt herself. Did you see her when she almost fell off the table? Hysterical!"

"No. I missed that."

"Conner's dad just got the pool opened up yesterday. Doesn't it look great? I feel like jumping in!" She turned to Shane. "Hello. Having a good time?" She reached over and touched his forearm, smiling with raised eyebrows as though she were bestowing a blessing on an imbecile. To confirm her impression, Shane grinned and nodded. I turned up my glass.

There are gaps in my mind from this point on. Conner brought us more drinks, I think. And we chatted for a few more minutes there by the pool, before the others began to find their way onto the patio. It seemed that Conner wanted to escape the crowd, their loud laughter and horseplay, or maybe he wanted to keep me and Shane for his and Jennifer's amusement. Anyway, we ended up in the pool house, just the four of us.

The front part was a lobby, providing shade, showers, and comfortable seating. Conner led us through this area to another doorway that opened into a private space: kitchenette, a cozy den with flat-screen on the wall, and a rec room with a pool table in the center.

"This is Conner's little hideaway," Jennifer explained. "We spend a lot of time here," she said with a smile. "It's like our own apartment. And Conner loves to play pool. Do you guys play—no, I don't imagine—but that's okay. Conner can show you. Anyone who can hold a stick can learn to play pool."

Shane and I sat on a brown leather loveseat. Conner was doing something in the kitchen. "I'm ready for a snack," he said. It's good to keep plenty in your stomach when you're drinking, you know. Dad taught me that. We can have a bite before we play."

Jennifer grabbed a remote from the top of a heavy glass table and pointed it at the TV. A reality show popped up, something about people who lived in the swamp and were always catching alligators and wrecking their trucks. "Oh my God," she said. "This show is freakin' hilarious! This family reminds me of people around here with their backward ways and country accents—oops. Not you, of course. I mean you guys know how to dress at least, and Colleen, like, you're really smart. So, obviously, all people who live out in the sticks aren't like these people, right? They are funny, though, with their ugly beards and camo everything. Conner, your show's on, baby. Looks like a new episode."

"Coming. I can't make the microwave go any faster."

Jennifer looked at me. "We can watch something else if you'd rather. This screen's like the one in the video room, hooked to a computer, so we've got the whole internet." She lowered her voice. "Sometimes we watch porn. Amazing. Wanna watch some porn?" Then she made a clucking sound with her tongue and slapped her forehead. "What was I thinking? That would be weird for you two."

"What would be weird?" Conner asked as he entered the room carrying a tray loaded with pizza-flavored, oozy pocket things on paper plates.

"Oh, nothing. I just had a random thought, about sex. You know what a dirty mind I have. I thought we could watch porn with Collie and Shane."

"What's weird about that?"

"They're cousins, silly. Weird, like sex between brother and sister."

Conner set the tray on the table. "Well, we *are* in Tanner County, Alabama. That's normal behavior here isn't it?" He and Jennifer laughed at his little joke.

"Conner, you're too *bad*!"

"No, really. That explains a lot about our senior class. Take a look at the results of all that inbreeding." He stepped over to the window across from us and pulled the curtain back slightly, exposing a scene of bedlam—our drunken classmates running around like idiots, whooping and hollering, chasing each other, and jumping into the pool with their clothes on. I caught a glimpse of Kristina climbing out, her wet shirt and shorts clinging to her. She laughed and squealed, and took off running from some guy. Then Conner closed the curtain.

"I hope nobody gets hurt," I said.

"They'll be fine," he said. "I imagine they'll start winding down pretty soon."

"Yeah, too bad all those stoner kids went to that other party," Jennifer said. "Some good weed would help us all to mellow out. Speaking of which, you still have some, don't you babe?"

"A little."

She turned to me with an inviting look. "What do you think? Wanna smoke some of Conner's weed?"

"Jennifer, you know I don't smoke that stuff."

Shane spoke up, his mouth full of pizza roll, lips red with sauce. "Naw, me neither."

"Well, I didn't know. I thought everybody did, at least once in a while."

Conner said, "That's okay, guys. I don't feel like being stoned now either. There would be one benefit, though. If we got really toasted, these gooey blobs would taste better."

I couldn't help but smile at this, and my darkening mood lightened. We stuffed our faces while the country-hick reality show played in the background. Conner refreshed our drinks and, when we were done with the pizza rolls, ushered us into the rec room.

The pool table rested under a hanging, stained-glass light. It was massive, with dark wood and deep leather pockets. Chairs were set around the perimeter, racks on the wall held sticks. In one corner of the room an old-school pinball machine beckoned, its lighted backboard displaying a gypsy girl in skimpy harem clothes under the garishly printed words, "Star Gazer." There was a juke box in another corner. This room was what I imagined a pool hall from back in the day would feel like, probably a tribute to Mr. Evans's youth.

I felt a little woozy. I remember setting another fresh drink on a table as Conner showed me how to hold the cue stick and make a proper bridge with my left hand. He had his arm around me to demonstrate. It didn't feel too bad.

"That's it," he said. "You're catching on. You've got to pump the stick with nice, smooth strokes. You make the shot two or three times before you actually shoot. Get it? You pump the stick to get the *feel* of making it without actually hitting the cue ball. Then, when everything's right, you just follow through. It happens when it happens—sort of unexpected."

He was talking into my ear and I felt his breath on my neck.

Jennifer cleared her throat loudly. "Well, let's rack, 'em up and play, shall we? What'll it be, eight ball? We can play partners." She grabbed Shane's hand. "Come on, big guy. Let's find you a stick."

The game didn't go well from the beginning. Conner, after racking the balls, insisted that Shane break them, even though he was wobbly and awkward with the stick. We were all giving him instructions, which added to his discomfort. He miscued, nearly ripping the felt. Jennifer said, "Careful, dude!" Then she urged Conner to give him another chance. I saw them wink at each other.

"That's okay," Conner said. "No harm done. Try again. You'll soon get the hang of it."

Shane said, "Naw. Maybe you should just go ahead. I don't—"

"No, no. I insist. Let's move the ball a little closer this time. Just keep your eye on it and follow through."

Shane finally managed to strike the cue cleanly enough to drive it into the racked balls and disperse them a little. Jennifer said, "Way to go partner! I knew you could do it!"

Conner took his turn and immediately started showing off with polished technique, driving the balls farther apart, pocketing five solids before just missing a bank shot in the side pocket. I thought, big deal. I'd actually played pool before with Dad. One of his friends had a table in his basement, not nearly as nice as Conner's, but serviceable. Dad's friend was good. I imagined if he were here, he'd show Conner a thing or two. I leaned on my stick waiting for Jennifer to take her turn.

"Don't worry, partner," she said, prissing around the table. "I'll get us back in the game." She rubbed against Shane, sliding past him in his chair. Looking waxy and pale, he glanced at me then turned away. Jennifer took forever preparing for her shot, aiming and pumping the stick. She was right in front of Shane, her ass in his face. I saw the fear in his eyes before it happened. He couldn't get up. He managed to turn but not enough. The sound was horrible as vomit splattered Jennifer's shapely calves and sandaled feet.

When she realized what had happened she dropped her stick and screamed, "What the fuck! You stupid retard. Oh my God! Stupid, hick retard can't even drink. You should stay in the woods where you came from. Conner! Conner! Do something—"

A dark filter dropped between me and the horror, slowing everything down and creating an illusory realm where only vengeance mattered, where my rage would make things right. The stick in my hand became a bat. There was Jennifer's hateful face before me, hanging high and outside, right where I liked it. It felt practiced and automatic, my perfect home run swing. The connection sent a gratifying current back through the stick into my arms. Then she was on the floor, her hair in Shane's vomit, her mouth a bubbling red hole.

A silent fog enveloped everything for half a second, until my stick clattered against the floor, dispelling the haze and exposing the broken shards of reality. Shane, on his hands and knees in the vomit and blood—pitifully reaching toward Jennifer—looked at me with a depth of sadness in his eyes I'd never seen. Then Conner slammed me into the wall in his anger and haste to help his girlfriend. Dread and disbelief pressed me to the floor. Bile rose in my throat, but I swallowed it down and managed not to vomit.

I retreated into a black void, but I couldn't stay there. Conner must have gone for help. I heard voices: rising shouts. People jostling. Hands everywhere, reaching for me, grabbing, pushing, pulling. Screams and sobs. I lost Shane. He must've run outside into the darkness. Absorbed by the crowd, I was shuffled and prodded to the patio. Then adults, concerned and angry, took over amid flashing lights. Jennifer was carried out on a stretcher, a bloody gauze pressed to her mouth. Conner, clinging to her hand, walked alongside to the ambulance.

Everyone was angry, shouting and cursing, except for Kristina. She pushed through the mob, her face wet with tears, her hair still wet from the pool. She reached out to me, but a policeman blocked her as two others cuffed my hands. Kristina followed as I was taken upstairs, but they wouldn't let her come inside the small wood-paneled room. Mr. Evans was there with his arms crossed over his chest. An older, heavier policeman pushed me down into a leather chair. They asked me all sorts of questions about what happened and who I was—had I even been invited, where were my parents, what drugs had I taken, who was the boy I had been with and where did he go—until they finally gave up, realizing I wasn't going to say a word.

When they opened the door, the crowd was gone. Only Mrs. Evans and Kristina, who had managed to change into dry clothes, remained. They sat, sad and serious, on a plush gray sofa, their hands in their laps until they saw me emerge. Kristina stood. The policeman let her walk beside me to the car. She rubbed my shoulder and stroked my hair. When he reached to open the door, she said, "It's okay, baby. Everything's gonna be all right."

I don't remember what I said or if I replied at all. I was glad she was there, but I didn't believe her. I knew I'd ruined our plans, that we wouldn't be going to Auburn together. But she would go. She'd find a great roommate, some cool chick from India or New York or somewhere, and she'd make lots of new friends and have a wonderful life.

In the back of the police car, as we rolled out of Conner's gated community, my thoughts turned to Shane. I imagined him in the woods, taking the short route back to his truck. He was safest in the woods, and I felt he would make it home okay, especially with the full moon. But later, what would he do? I hoped I wouldn't have to stay in jail long. I needed to get back to him and our rightful place.

I thought about what I would say at the police station when they started questioning me again. I would have to talk eventually to them and my parents. My mind swelled, buzzing with things I suddenly knew that I'd really known all along about Shane, Rayford, and Aunt Polly—old knowledge brought to light alongside new knowledge—and I also thought about what I wouldn't say, what would stay forever locked inside me.

As the radio squawked and tires hummed, I remembered Rayford over the years with his white hair and bleak expression. The Lord's dealing with him, I'd often said to myself, content with letting it go at that. But now I knew the agony he had caused had been squared, finally made right. The Lord's work? I don't know about that.

The answer solidified to the nagging question of how, after Rayford's solemn prohibitions, Shane had managed to take part in the graduation night festivities. We now faced a host of new problems stemming from his actions. I was too preoccupied earlier to think about it, but when I remembered his phone call and later how he'd stood up to Conner at the restaurant, I understood what Shane had done to get away from his daddy. Past sins ripple onto present shores, bringing new horrors. I was glad he had an alibi, and I had confidence in his abilities, his knowledge of abandoned roads and trails.

Things would be complicated for a while, my trouble along with, after all these years, another disappearance and investigation. Mom and Dad, MawMaw and PawPaw would be sad and disappointed, but they would understand and support us. Soon I'd be with Shane and we could all help each other. That's what families are for. I looked out the window at the moon and stars, a beautifully clear night. On the horizon I could see our hills.

INERTIA

WHILE AMERICA WAS CALLING her troops home from Vietnam, Ty Ragsdale was spending lots of time at the Billy Goat Bar. He was winning a game of eight ball one evening when he noticed a stocky young man in the corner, drinking alone and watching him. The man had close-cropped hair, prematurely receded. He wore jeans, flannel shirt, and boots. By the looks of his hands and forearms he could have been a house framer or a mason.

Ty had spent the previous Saturday night at another man's home, and now he was alert to the eyes of this stranger. The woman had told him about the separation and impending divorce, but he had been aware, in the midst of his pleasure, of a lingering male presence. As he chalked up and pretended to survey the next shot, he watched peripherally the man approaching with balled fists. When Ty heard the voice—"Hey, Ragsdale"—he was already turning, shifting his grip on the cue stick. With both hands on the small end, he swung it like a baseball bat from a hurried stance. The advancing man took the blow under his left arm.

The cue seemed to find lodgment in the man's ribs. Actually, the cuckold's rage had kept his reflexes sharp; he dropped his arm and grabbed the big end of the stick, gaining the advantage, which Ty was quick to realize.

Rather than lose the pulling contest, Ty turned the shorter man's strength against him by stepping in with a hard elbow to his mouth. As the man's fingers loosened, Ty planted and jerked back, regaining his weapon. The next blow was an abbreviated punch. The fat handle struck the forehead sharply, making the sound of a popped cork. His head snapped back, but the husband managed to keep his balance and bring his fists up. Ty's stick found the bridge of his nose, even though it was partially blocked by forearms. Ty stopped the husband's arm-flailing counter attack, a paroxysm of pain and rage, with a quick jab of the stick into his Adam's apple. The man's hands went to his throat as his tongue protruded from his red mouth. The next blow cracked against his left cheekbone. As he reeled backwards, the head was an easy target, which Ty was quick to find with the stick. This downward stroke brought the battered husband to his knees. A rapid succession of chopping blows followed. Ty swung the cue from a workman's stance as if hoeing out a drought-hardened corn row, striking shoulders, neck, arms, and hands as his defeated opponent tried in vain to protect himself. Ty kept swinging until the husband was face-down with his hands over his head, moaning and bleeding from his busted mouth and nose onto the gritty floor.

A bystander finally caught the stick as Ty was bringing it back for yet another blow. "Awright now," he said in Ty's ear. "He's beat. You got him. Lemme have the stick."

The spectators' circle changed shape. More hands took hold of the cue, and someone managing a hasty half-nelson on Ty's left side said in a high, excited voice, "It's over, it's over."

Ty bucked and strained against them as the larger world came into focus. He jerked his head from side to side, surveying the crowd as they watched, mouths gaping; then he relented, releasing the stick without completely releasing his anger. They loosened their grip as he stopped straining. He blurted out, "What's wrong with that son of a bitch! What's his damn problem!" Then he broke free, stepped over the man he had beaten, and walked out the back door.

It was a cooler than normal evening for early summer, but Ty didn't notice. He mounted his big, straight-piped Honda, a motorcycle he referred to as the "Beast," and ripped out of the parking lot. He rode hard past the town limits onto a familiar, curvy back road, searching for his rhythm of accelerating and backing off, leaning into the turns, concentrating on handling the machine. Suddenly, as he came over a hill into a little hollow and began to lean into the next curve, the world turned ghostly white. He was in the middle of a dense patch of fog, traveling at a high rate of speed into a curve that had disappeared.

There was no guiding line at the edge of the blacktop, and his eyes only vaguely discerned the shape of a rising bank to his right. He put out his left foot when his wheels dropped off the pavement. The rough shoulder hammered him, and the bike's suspension bounced him up onto the gas tank. Unidentified shapes rushed by on his right. The bike dipped and rose violently as he crossed the ditch and started up the embankment. He was still upright somehow when the fog passed, revealing the gaping black hole of a fast-approaching metal culvert where the ditch ran under a gravel driveway. Farther up the embankment to his right, the surface broke up into boulder-strewn gullies. It was all or nothing: at the limit of what he and the machine could do—left foot dragging the ground, leaning at an impossibly sharp, footpeg-scraping angle—he passed just to the left of death's sharp edge.

Another bounce put him back on the pavement, able to see again. A wave of nausea coursed through him, forcing him to pull over and yank off his helmet. Trembling from the unceasing expenditure of effort—from his first swing of the cue stick until now as he tried not to vomit after seeing death's black void and struggling to steer the Beast away from it—Ty decided to slow down and to stay away from the Billy Goat Bar for a while.

Somehow he was still alive and free. A sense of relief, borne on the cool night air, washed him as he rode. It was similar to a feeling he had had once before at a high school dance his cousin Toby had persuaded him to attend. He had no business there, having dropped out of school the previous spring, goaded by Coach Thompson and his grudge over Ty's quitting football. There would have been a fight that night had it not been for a pretty girl and her peaceful aspect. He replayed those details from over a year ago and thought about her face as he rode.

Ty had first approached the girl filled with his usual confidence. She had been mock-dancing with her girlfriends, swaying, shimmying, acting silly to "In-A-Gadda-Da Vida," being cranked out by a local band. He had picked her out of the group, noticing her thick hair and spirited movements, and when she looked, he offered a smile. She averted her eyes, redirecting her attention to her friends and the fun they were having. When the song finally ended, Ty approached them in their laughter and said to the one he had singled out, "I like the way you dance."

Once again she looked away, threw her arm around a girlfriend's shoulders. "Come on Becky, let's go get a Coke." They turned their backs on Ty and vanished into the crowd. He stood perplexed in a pocket of people he didn't know. He looked for Toby but couldn't locate him before the band launched into their next song, "Sunshine of Your Love." People jammed onto the floor and began flailing about as they gave themselves over to the beat.

Ty, knocked off his rhythm, sought the safety of the sidelines, where the shy and clumsy sat in metal chairs or leaned against the wall. He pulled a Winston from his shirt pocket, stuck it to his lip, and made his way around the room. He wanted to step outside to smoke and think about that girl. As he cut across the corner to the exit, he felt an arm on his shoulder. He turned, expecting Toby or some other friendly face; instead, he found himself looking into the glaring visage of Coach Thompson, his old nemesis who had poked him in the chest that day in front of the whole class. The man shouted over the racket, his face inches from Ty's, "You can't smoke in here, Ragsdale."

"It ain't lit," Ty shouted back.

"Well, if you go outside, you can't come back in."

"Why not? I paid my money like everybody else."

"Because that's the rule. Besides, you're not supposed to be here anyway. This dance is for students."

"Coulda fooled me—I thought it was for losers, like yourself."

"That's it, Ragsdale, you're outta here! We're not gonna put up with trouble makers."

Ty jerked away when Coach Thompson grabbed the back of his arm. "Get your damned hands off me." The kids around them stopped dancing, eager for excitement. Ty felt eyes on him as he and Coach squared off. The jutting, stubbled chin and yellow teeth brought back that day in history class when Coach had embarrassed him, making a big deal over that stupid World War II project. He should have whipped his ass then instead of storming out as he'd done. Now he scanned the faces that were looking at him and locked for an instant on a pair of intense blue eyes, those of the girl with thick hair.

Coach said, "You'll do what I say, Ragsdale, or wish you had."

There was a dark closet in Ty's mind filled with memories of his mom and dad's fights, the slapping sounds, the shouts and curses, and his own pain at having his drunk father's quick hand against his ear. Those days were gone, but sometimes, still, things happened that caused the closet door to fly open, releasing a rush of foul-smelling tormentors—dark creatures who, with black wings flapping, altered his perceptions—but now the girl's blue eyes shone through the swaying shadows. She looked at Ty intently for only a second, just long enough for him to return the gaze and notice the barely perceptible movement of her head saying earnestly to him alone, "No."

He turned his attention back to the bristled little man before him, who now seemed ridiculous. Ty took a deep breath. "Sure coach, I'll leave. I don't want no trouble." As he turned to go, he sought the girl's face again. Their eyes met, and he picked up the shy smile before she turned back to her friends.

Ty drove home with his head full of fantasies. He felt as if he had been cleansed and redeemed by the experience; radiant vistas opened up, reducing the strain of life and its grimy meanness. As time passed, the girl's number in his wallet—procured through the detective efforts of cousin Toby—became a seed of hope.

At work the night after the bar fight, Ty learned that the man was okay. Several customers had lifted him up, washed his face, and got him to his truck. He wasn't a regular, so no one knew what happened after, except that he had made it out of the parking lot under his own power. The fight was the main break room topic for several nights, and Ty sensed the growing respect of the men at the plant. He feigned indifference about the beaten man's condition and managed not to show that he was sick and worried about possible repercussions.

One of the machine operators, a large-hipped boy who worked alongside Ty, was fascinated with the story. Bowman ran a die press, as did Ty, but without his counterpart's grace and fluidity. Night after night Ty stamped out more perfect, shiny parts than did Bowman, seemingly with ease, never hurrying and forgetting important steps in the process. Bowman did not show outward jealousy of his more able co-worker, but rather a fawning admiration. He kept pressing for details about the fight.

"So you caught him right in the Adam's apple, huh? That's a pretty amazing shot with a cue stick! Was that the turning point in the fight, do you think? Was that when you knew you had him?"

"You know, it all happened so fast, I really don't remember."

"Some of the guys said he had a knife, that he came at you with a knife."

"Naa. He didn't have no knife."

"That's what they're saying, that he came at you from out of nowhere with a knife and before he knew what was what, you was all over him with that cue stick, beating him like a yard dog."

"He was just coming, that's all."

Conversation usually took place in the break room. This particular night, however, Bowman's machine was down for repairs. He was supposed to be helping Ty with a set-up, changing dies and feeder settings on his machine for a new run of parts. He wasn't much help because of his incessant chatter, and the set-up was taking too long. Finally Millwood, the foreman, came over. He was a tall, slender man in his forties, angular and slightly stooped. With him standing there watching, Bowman kept talking.

"Who was that guy anyway? Why do you think he wanted to jump you?"

"I don't know. I think he had me mixed up with somebody else."

"You sure about that, Ty?" Millwood interjected. "You think that man jumped you for no reason, 'cause he was crazy or something?"

"I don't know what his damn problem was. I just know I wasn't gon' stand there and wait for an explanation."

"So you attacked him with a stick."

"He was the one doing the attacking, I was just defending myself."

"Did he ever even hit you?"

"Hell, I didn't give him the chance. But he was coming at me, fists balled up, mad as hell 'bout something."

Bowman listened, hanging on every word. The older man said, "You ever seen two tomcats fight, Ragsdale? They fight to protect their territory. They're protective of what's theirs. Men are the same way, except they take their mates for life. It ain't no seasonal thing like with animals, and it's their duty to fight to keep some tomcat from taking what belongs to them. Marriage means something, boy. Didn't you know that?"

Ty looked down at the dismantled machinery. "She told me they was getting a divorce, that he wasn't around."

"She was a married woman, and that fella you beat up with a stick—her husband—happens to be a friend of mine. He ain't been able to work since it happened. He's hurting on the inside more than from all the bruises that stick left. He's a good man who tries to do what's right, and I ain't so sure it woulda turned out like it did if you hadn't had that stick."

Bowman's eyes twitched as he followed the conversation. Ty, unable to look Millwood in the face, studied the fit of the parts as the older man spoke. "You ain't gotta worry about me, Ragsdale. Everything's strictly business between us. I'm gonna treat you like everybody else, but I will say this: you better watch yourself. You better be careful where you go and what you mess around with. Now, if this machine ain't up and running in ten minutes, I'm gonna send both of you home. I don't want to hear no more talk about beating people with sticks and screwing their wives. I just ain't in the mood for it. Is that clear?"

Words of protest were forming on Ty's lips as he raised his face to answer, but when he saw the drawn brow of the foreman and the sharp features, he dropped his eyes. "Yessir."

Millwood left then and Bowman and Ty resumed their work, tapping the steel guides and dies into place and locking them down with their Allen wrenches. They worked without speaking, except for an occasional muttering from Bowman. After a while, Ty asked, "What did you say?"

"Oh, nothing. I just didn't know you'd been doing his wife."

Ty didn't feel like answering. In fact, he didn't feel as if he could continue working because of the sharp cramping in his gut. He waited long enough for Millwood to be on the other side of the plant, then left his post. The cramping caused him to step quickly. He felt that something vile and forbidden was boiling deep in his insides.

The lighting was different in the restroom where the stench and relative quiet signaled relief to his muscles. He was barely able to make it to the toilet before everything let go. There wasn't even time to wipe off the seat.

Relief came in convulsive waves as a hot brown river jetted from his insides. He expelled an inordinate amount of putrescent waste, and he wondered if his organs had rotted away and dissolved into the lumpy, stinking flood rising beneath him. Then it was over. Depleted, he trembled on the seat, alone with the stench of his bowels and the hum of the flickering light. He rubbed his head, pushing the sweat on his brow back with the hair that had fallen across his face. His eyes were drawn then to the vulgar scrawlings on the stall partition.

Obscenities were piled on top of one another, and he read them half expecting to find his name. He saw that other name then, written in a neater script that made it stand apart: "Jesus loves you and can save you from your sins." It was a puzzling thought that lingered as he went back to work, feeling much better.

The remainder of Ty's shift ran out smoothly with no more talk of the fight. His head was empty except for a newly developed wariness as he walked out of the plant into the streaked and varied hues of a lingering sunrise. He noticed the morning colors as he wiped the dew off the seat and gas tank of the Honda with the hand towel he kept in the tool compartment. Above the horizon lazy clouds floated; he supposed they looked like something, but he had no idea what. Their shapes represented nothing other than drifting, poorly defined smudges that were, for the moment, turned orange and glorified by the sun. The clouds remained before him on the horizon, holding their color as he rode eastward, toward home and much-needed rest.

He still had the blue-eyed girl's number in his wallet. For some reason, though, picking up the phone was difficult, like beginning a project without all the materials. It was easier not to start. But he still planned to call someday, and as he rode his mechanical beast into the morning, he thought about what he would say.

I SANK THE MANDOLIN

WATER IN THE COVE so smooth it seems congealed until a soft breeze produces a fluid response, a subtle procession of ripples. I can no longer enjoy this scene that had, before I sank the mandolin, always provided serenity of spirit. I watched the instrument as it slowly descended toward the channel's rocky shelf, eternity's hard floor. My eyes followed the shape of the curved, hollow body, stuffed through the sound hole with rocks, growing smaller as it dropped into darkness. After I broke the neck I wanted it gone, out of sight, and so it was. Yea, she dropped through the valley of cold dark death, and now I fear all evil, especially when I imagine the water of the cove on a calm spring day.

I couldn't play the damned thing even though I tried for years. Inscrutable instrument of paired strings, difficult, almost yielding yet remaining stiff-necked, frustrating to my fingers and soul. Father had planned my future for as long as I can remember: I would be the mandolin player in our family group, preserving the old music (with our own unique interpretations) for future generations, an honorable calling he had assured me. We had the fiddle, banjo, bass, and guitar; the mandolin had always been lacking, and it was my destiny, after my mother and sisters took up their parts, to fill this void. I tried, probably harder than Father ever knew. But how can we know what another perceives, even our own flesh and blood? Father may have known, but it doesn't matter now. The end result is the same: rejection and alienation, even from the brotherhood of man.

Father's preaching convinced me that through faith all things were possible, and for a while I made progress. I learned the melodies but couldn't play them well enough, my fingers too fat for the narrow fret spaces, my picking too slow. The demands of my marriage, which came late to a woman Father approved of, overwhelmed my need and desire to practice. Years of stagnation, followed by disappointment and shame. After slowly abandoning the rectitude of persistence, I began to harbor visions of the act: the snapping of the neck, disposing of the body. This period in my mind is a smeared stretch of torment. There were times of penitent heart when I would pick up my old instrument yet again, telling myself I couldn't give up while knowing I already had.

The actual event came suddenly, a seamless blending of thought and action, subconscious and conscious realities wafting into one sublime moment—crack! There it was: broken instrument on the unswept floor, a stinging under my eye, a dull throb above my knee. My mind lurched. Compelled to look at myself, I shuddered at my face in the mirror. Blood on my cheek. Thin skin sliced by snapped E string. The last pain it would ever inflict! Now by God it was over, almost. I daubed the blood away, not much really. Gathered her up, headstock hanging, and walked the familiar, rock-strewn trail to the cove whose bottom I had never been able to reach.

I had often dived into that water when I was young and strong, swimming down into cold darkness until my ears hurt and fear sent me back up. My broken instrument would find the bottom I had felt for. Rocks would ensure a steady sinking. The surface undulated, welcoming the weighted body.

I watched the slow descent for a long time, expecting something—revelation, a new mood, clarity of thought—but nothing came except a shuddering of my frame, unaccountable after such a simple act yet real, making me feel as though my soul were leaving. I had sought change, an end to the frustration, but the difference is different from what I had imagined. I am hollow now, like the body of my broken instrument, and there is no freedom.

Father's expectations forged an unbreakable bond. Through fate and blood the die is cast, and we are imprisoned in spite of all we can muster of ourselves. I look at my idle hands, stupid cursed fingers, and gaze out this window at the bright spring sky. My mind spins into the blue and returns to that day at the cove.

I finally looked up, after she'd sunk beneath my vision. Ducks were there on the far side, gliding on a liquid mirror. A hawk circled overhead. I absorbed the scene with its rush of sound—the breeze in the tender leaves, birds twittering, squirrels scampering, crickets, frogs, the splash of a jumping fish, a distant outboard motor. Nothing and everything had changed. A drab patina, emanating from my putrefied core, now covered all. I turned away trembling.

I can't go there anymore, except through the window in my mind. When I do—and sometimes it's unavoidable—the shudder returns, but lighter now. Each time lighter for there's not much left. I am hollow and broken, locked inside a cold, dark space where the floor's grit aggravates and the iron-laden water leaves permanent brown stains.

OPERATING EXPENSES

RANDY WAS WATCHING the Munich Summer Olympics on the snowy black and white portable he had recently bought at the pawn shop. This was the second full day of competition, and he thought he would relax for a while before loading his backpack and heading out. He wasn't in any hurry to start hitchhiking again.

As he settled into the lumpy recliner, he was roused by the sound of tires on gravel and the honking of a car horn. He looked through the window to see who it was and immediately recognized the car and its occupant. Mrs. Bea Stempton, newly widowed, had driven her dead husband's Ford Galaxie right up to the front of the lopsided old shack. She honked the horn again before he could find a decent shirt to put on. As he stepped out onto the porch, she called to him through the passenger window: "Come on, you can drive me back and keep the car for a while, until we can get the flatbed going."

Randy blinked and stammered. "I wasn't planning on … I was getting ready to—"

"I know. We ain't had a chance to talk, with the funeral and everything. Just get in and drive. I'll explain when we get to the house. Stacy's there waiting on us."

Mrs. Stempton began rummaging in her purse as soon as they were under way. "You'll need gas, oil, and a new chain for the saw. This should hold you for a week or so. Let me know when you need more." Randy was surprised to see that she was offering him a hundred dollar bill, shaking it impatiently. "Go on, take it," she said. "It's for operating expenses."

～

THE NEXT MORNING, the second day after Mr. Stempton's funeral, Randy was up before daylight. Troubling thoughts had visited him there in the shack during that long, sleepless night. Mrs. Stempton and her daughter, Stacy, needed him to continue working to finish out a contract made before the accident. Stacy's brother was useless to them, having sought and found a different way of life in Atlanta. As they'd discussed the matter over coffee in the kitchen of the old home place, Stacy's tears and sad smile had been persuasive, obscuring the fact that she shared an apartment in town with her boyfriend. She had said, "Randy, we—I—need you to stay. *Please?*" Her hair was the color of broom straw caught in a sunset and her eyes were startling, like a clear sky at dawn after a storm. Now, alone in the morning's stillness, Randy realized that she only saw him as a friend who could help the family in their time of need, and he felt foolish and weak for having agreed to stay.

Other concerns centered mainly around pulling stumps and clearing land, but as he began to order things in his mind, he realized that the pulpwood must be cut and hauled first. This part of the job was familiar to him, having worked for weeks as Ben Stempton's helper, but instead of bringing comfort, trying to picture the details produced greater anxiety. The pulpwood truck and saws would be where the old man had left them. Randy would have to begin where Ben Stempton ended to finish out the load.

It was hard to believe the old man was dead. The memory was still fresh of the lumbering, loaded truck pulling over to the side of the road on that hot afternoon to offer him, stumbling under his heavy backpack, a ride. He remembered Ben's face: the opaque blue eyes looking him up and down, the grizzled whiskers stained brown around the mouth from tobacco juice.

He had asked, "Where ya headed, boy?" Surely he'd sensed that Randy had no place to go. He'd even seemed to know—though he couldn't have—about his past in the Pittsburgh orphanage and the foster homes, a past Randy was trying to forget. The old man had recognized an opportunity, but so had Randy. He had been at the limit of his endurance; being free was not working out as he'd expected. Realizing he didn't have much to lose, he accepted the offer of work and an abandoned shack to live in. He had not planned to stay long, but working with Mr. Stempton—cutting and loading pulpwood, dragging the fragrant pine tops out of the way, sweating, swatting flies—was satisfying. The old man provided lunch daily, and each evening he delivered to the shack a hot, tinfoil-wrapped supper plate piled high by Mrs. Stempton: fried pork chops or chicken, boiled cabbage, beans, squash, and sliced tomatoes with mashed potatoes or fried okra. It was a good enough set-up, at least until he could think of something else. Days turned into weeks, summer faded, and the old man got killed.

Now, the nature of the accident and the unknown details made the thought of beginning his day's labor at the scene of a grisly death repugnant, and he groped for a means of escape. Weighing his limited options in the light of Stacy's smile and Mrs. Stempton's kindness, he concluded that he should do what he had promised to do, even as he clung to a fading image of himself as a free man, an adventurous drifter, loving a string of women along life's highway.

Mrs. Stempton was waiting for him when he pulled into the yard, an apron tied around her ample midsection.

She handed him his day's sustenance—breakfast and lunch packed carefully inside a grocery sack rolled down tight—from the front porch steps. "Good morning," she said. "I'm pleased to see you out bright and early. I went ahead and got everything ready 'cause I knew you'd want to get started."

Randy returned the greeting, took the package. Mrs. Stempton's manner in handing him the sack didn't invite conversation, and there was nothing else to talk about anyway. If she shared his discomfort with where he was going and what had happened there, she didn't show it. Perhaps, he thought, her mind was incapable of going into such dark places.

The Jenkins property was just outside of Prathersville on Taylor's Gin Road. He covered the six miles slowly, savoring his breakfast: a sausage biscuit as big as a cat's head with sweet creamed coffee from a thermos. He decided to try the radio, pressing each of the buttons, but found only country and gospel music amid the static. Using the tuning knob to explore between the presets, he stumbled upon Don McLean's "American Pie." He hadn't heard it since before he left Pittsburgh, when it was still at the top of the charts. Hearing it rekindled his wanderlust.

He drove up to the rough access road with the lyrics in his head and noticed that the pulpwood truck was visible from the main blacktop to anyone who happened to be looking. He turned in and stopped the Ford a short distance behind the truck, which was loaded with only one layer of fat logs across its frame-mounted rack. He sat there trying to discern what he could from the car's insulated interior. With the truck positioned at an angle to the access road and the loader boom with its cable swung around to the far side, Randy could see nothing out of the ordinary. The rising sun made shadows, distorted images of leaves and limbs, sway and dance across the hood of the car. He told himself that it might not be that bad. Maybe the people who took the old man away had cleaned everything up. He was reaching for the door handle when he heard a vehicle approaching from behind.

In the mirror, Randy watched the front end of a polished Lincoln grow larger, dipping and rebounding in a constrained fashion over the driveway's harsh bumps. He could make out two occupants, a man on the passenger side and what appeared to be a teenage boy behind the wheel. Randy grew apprehensive, wondering if he had broken some law, as the ponderous vehicle pulled within a few feet of the Ford's back bumper.

The man got out first and then the boy, who lagged behind as if waiting for instructions. Randy opened the door and stepped out. The figure approaching him wore baggy trousers, suspenders, and a white shirt. The stub of a wet, well-chewed cigar protruded from his slack mouth and his receding gray hair was pushed straight back. His rounded shoulders belied the initial impression of substance imparted by his bulky midsection, which, Randy noticed as the man drew nearer, consisted entirely of soft flab.

He regarded Randy through narrowed eyes and shifted the cigar to one side with lips and tongue. "Hello there, young man. You must be Ben Stempton's boy."

"Well, no. I just work for him. I'm supposed to pick up where he left off."

"You mean here, on this property?"

"Yessir. To finish out the job. That's what Mrs. Stempton and I decided."

"Y'all did, huh? I'm glad you got everything worked out, but you might of informed me, since I own this piece o' land. Name's Wayne Jenkins, and I'm the one who's already paid Ben Stempton to clear this place off. Who are you? When I made the deal with Ben, I figured ol' Buena was still working for him. He didn't say nothing about no white boy."

"I'm Randy Walls, from Pittsburgh."

The man appraised Randy's appearance as he worked the cigar slowly to the other side of his mouth with his tongue and lips. "That sure was bad about Ben. Who woulda thought it. I didn't know he had relatives from up north."

"We're not related. I just work for him. Met him about a month ago."

Mr. Jenkins looked down as if studying out a problem, and Randy noticed his fancy cowboy boots. His young driver was smoking a cigarette, leaning against the Lincoln.

"An old lady found him, Miss Elmira Tuggle," the man said. "She was going to the grocery store and happened to look up this way. I imagine it was real unnatural, seeing ol' Ben squeezed up against them truck standards, hanging like a tater sack cinched in the middle. She called the deputies, and then I heard it on my scanner. They was getting him down when I got here. A real mess and a damn shame too." He made this point while removing the wet stub from his mouth and examining it as if there were some mysterious connection between its ruined carcass and Ben Stempton's. Randy noticed a fleck of black tobacco on his tongue.

"So you were here when they took Mr. Stempton's body away?"

"Yep. I watched 'em load him up. And I can tell you it's nothing short of a miracle what Dougherty's funeral home was able to do. I never figured they'd open that casket, but they did and I know it was a comfort to Mrs. Stempton. Anyway, that's over and done with. The rest of us has got to keep going. Ain't that right?"

"Yessir, I believe so. That's what I'm trying to do."

"We've got to keep working and planning and making things happen, and what I'm trying to make happen is a small subdivision, about twenty-five or thirty houses. I think they ought to sit real nice in here, that is if I can get the property cleared off so the builders can start puttin' in the footings. I need to get them houses dried-in before the weather turns cold and rainy."

The man examined both ends of the cigar stub thoughtfully then flipped it to the ground. Randy waited for the point that Mr. Jenkins seemed to be working toward, but instead of speaking he crossed his arms over his chest, shifted his weight, and began craning his neck, taking a slow visual sampling of each direction. Randy recognized this as a cue for him to offer something.

"Mrs. Stempton and I have discussed everything. We're going to honor the deal."

"I was thinking of paying Bea a visit to see where things stood, but, of course, I'd have to give her a few days, the funeral being so recent and all. See, I've been debating whether or not to just go ahead and bring in the big loggers and bulldozers and get it done. I didn't figure she'd have any notions about finishing out the contract with Ben gone. Trouble is, that heavy equipment would tear this place up to where you wouldn't recognize it. I want to keep all these nice shade trees and preserve the natural beauty. Besides, bulldozers are too damn expensive. On the other hand, though, is this time thing. In the building business you're always fighting time. There's a lot at stake here, boy. I'm already committed—very committed—so I've got to make the right choices. You following me?"

"Yessir. But I'm here this morning to get started.... I feel sure I can keep the same schedule that you and Mr. Stempton agreed on."

Mr. Jenkins eyed Randy up and down, then motioned to the teenage boy waiting back at the Lincoln. "Bring me a cigar, Lyle. They's some in the dash." The boy responded quickly and was soon at Mr. Jenkins' side, holding before him like a talisman a fat brown blunt, still in its cellophane. Randy rested his weight against the back of the Ford as

Mr. Jenkins tore off the wrapper and dropped it to the ground. He examined the cigar and worried over its closed end while Lyle fished in his pocket for a lighter. After nibbling off the stump and licking the cigar along its entire length, Mr. Jenkins was ready for his smoke. The teenager produced the lighter and held the flame at the glowing tip for several seconds while the man worked his cheeks, producing thick balls of aromatic smoke that hung about his head in an expanding festoon. After Lyle clanked shut the lighter, Randy, sensing that the boy was looking at him, turned his head, shifting his gaze to the pulpwood truck.

Mr. Jenkins said through the dissipating cloud, "You know, the deputies sure were puzzled about what happened to Ben. They just couldn't see how he managed to get that cable wrapped around him thataway."

Randy worked a weed out from the ground with the toe of his boot. "I've thought about it—wondered, I mean. The old man, he could do anything. But the cable's stiff and it's got some kinks in it that get twisted up sometimes. It's freaky, but it could happen. Hooking the cable and working the loader is really a two-man job. I would have been here helping, but—"

"You're right, boy. Unexplainable things happen all the time. Best not to worry too much over 'em."

Mr. Jenkins puffed knowingly on the cigar, as if pondering the wisdom of his words. Lyle, the teenager, looked at the man through the haze, then shifted his attention back to Randy, leaning uncomfortably against the trunk of the Ford.

"He said I could have a day off and I took it. I didn't know he was gonna...."

The man withdrew the cigar from his cheek. "I got some real concerns here, young man. I don't mind telling you. I knew Ben Stempton—what he was capable of—and he always kept his word. He'd been doing this kind of work all his life. But you … well, you seem like a fine young man, but I'm not sure you're up the task. You know what they say: never send a boy to do a man's job. What do you think? Can you clear off forty acres, haul out all the pine and brush and pull up the stumps by the end of October? That's what Ben and me agreed on. I can't afford to push it out no further."

Randy straightened himself. "I wouldn't have taken the job if I didn't believe I could do it."

"Uh-huh. Well, at least you got confidence. You'll need it. I don't know what you and Mrs. Stempton worked out, but there's quite a bit more money in this deal, that is if it gets done in time. And y'all are getting all of whatever the pulpwood brings. Did she tell you that?"

"Yessir."

"Well, awright then." He looked at Randy and nodded for several seconds before sticking the blunt back in his cheeks and puffing, just in time to bring the ember back to glowing life. "Looka here," he said through the smoke. He reached around to the bottom of his baggy trousers and brought out a fat billfold. After ceremoniously leafing through the bills, he picked a crisp hundred from the wad. "Here," he said, "some good faith money. And I got a suggestion. When you finish out this first load and take it in, look around and see if you can hire somebody to help. I know there's usually some young bucks hanging around that pulpwood yard looking for something to do. Think about it: one sawing, one loading. Another pair of hands to hook the cable around the logs and the chain around stumps. It'll make the job go a lot faster. Besides, with a helper, you won't be all by yourself out here."

He thrust the bill at him.

Randy was hesitant. He felt Lyle watching to see what he would do. "I think I'd rather wait until I've actually earned some money."

Mr. Jenkins shook the bill closer to his face. "Don't be a jackass. You'll earn it soon enough out here in this heat. And, like I said, there's plenty more where this came from—that is, so long as I see progress. I don't mind paying some each week. This'll be your first payment, and you can use part of it to hire you some help."

The tone of the man's voice, his impatient shaking of the bill, and the smoke about his head combined to make a forceful presence. Randy took the money as Lyle looked on with a blank, pleased expression.

"I'll stop by from time to time to see how things are going. I'll give it a week before I decide anything, you know, about the big loggers and bulldozers." Mr. Jenkins rocked back on his heels, looped his thumbs under his suspenders, and puffed as he waited for Randy's response.

"I'll do my best."

"That's all that can be expected, and I appreciate it. I've got a little better feeling about this now. I believe you'll do awright." As his cheeks pulled at the cigar, he offered a hand that felt to Randy, as he shook it, like a scaled and gutted carp.

"Come on, Lyle. We got other business this morning. You take care, young man—Randy wasn't it? Don't get too hot. We'll be seeing you later."

And that was that. Mr. Jenkins turned and walked back to his Lincoln with Lyle stepping lightly alongside. Then Randy was alone with the trees, vines, and briars in the surrounds of the partially loaded pulpwood truck and culpable cable. The moment of his facing what the old man left behind was at hand. As he lifted himself off the trunk of the car, he felt the crinkling bills in his pocket and realized he was in possession of more money than he had ever had in his life.

He waited until the Lincoln was out of sight then approached the other side of the truck circumspectly, hoping for the best, but the buzzing of flies presaged a disturbing reality. Dreading each step, he moved slowly until he was actually there where the life had spilled. At first he turned away gagging. The chorus of dollars in his pocket began to taunt, reminding him that he didn't have to do this, that they and the old man's Ford could take him away from this place. But a softer, smaller voice persisted through the prattle and told him he had to face it, a fact he accepted in his stomach where the churning was. Turning back was made bearable by a process he didn't understand, a knotting of something inside, accompanied by blue flashes in the outer realms of his consciousness— the bright morning sky glimpsed between swaying leaves, or the flickering glances of Stacy Stempton in his mind. As he faced the flies and the blood-soaked ground, spotted with chunks of dried and rotting organic matter, he was surprised at how easy it was. He told himself over and over, "This isn't so bad. It's not so bad. Not so bad…."

Then he was stepping over the spot of thickest clotting, where the flies, orgiastic, were loath to disperse. The cable was a mess, twisted up against the truck frame and kinked where Ben Stempton had died, smeared and stippled with daubs of flesh, tissue, and fabric. He opened the passenger door and reached in for one of the grease rags the old man always kept there. Before the cable could be rewound, it would have to be untangled and wiped down.

He set himself to the task, working the kinks out and rubbing the stiff metal cord. As he worked, time froze inside the hum of the flies. Finally, after starting the engine and winding the clean, straightened cable back onto its drum at the top of the standards, thought returned with urgency, telling him to move the truck away from that spot. The familiarity of the driver's seat, pedals, and gear lever brought relief.

He was able to move the rig only a hundred or so feet before he would have to clear out some brush and small pines, but at least he would be away from the stench and the flies. The truck seemed eager, unchanged by what had happened. As he engaged the clutch and began to roll over the rough terrain, he felt a loosening of the accident's hateful grip. The slow-rolling wheels pulled up a new scene with clean smells and sounds where Randy, through his muscles, could shape a different reality. He pushed the nagging thoughts of problems and expenses out of his mind, hopped down from the cab, and reached for the saw. Using his foot to keep it steady on the ground, he fingered the choke knob and yanked the cord.

BARBECUE

ME AND JOHNNY'S going to The Hickory Hut for smoky charred pork slathered with sweet vinegar sauce, Brunswick stew, creamy cole slaw, and buttered Texas toast. We've got the evening to kill before we clock in on the graveyard shift at Weinraub Manufacturing, and we're happy over not having to go to Viet Nam. The lottery results have just been announced and our numbers are both high, 274 and 302. Hot damn! We beat it.

Johnny's '64 Impala with new headers and glasspack mufflers sounds strong cruising down Highway 61. I can tell he's itching to let it out on the Hominy Creek stretch, but as we come around the curve before the half-mile straightaway, we see flashing lights down near the bridge. The V8 pops and cackles as Johnny takes his foot off of it.

"Shit," he says, "what's happened down there?"

"I don't know. Guess we'll find out."

As we approach, we see two Georgia state trooper cars. The sheriff's department and the police are there with lights flashing. The whole highway's blocked.

Johnny turns off onto a little dirt road, slides to a stop, kills the engine. I look at him. "Might as well see what's going on," he says. We hop out and start jogging toward the commotion.

Cars are pulling off onto the shoulders. People, clustering at the bridge, shout and point down into the gully. State troopers holding clipboards study the shoulder of the road, look up and down the highway and over the bridge into the creek. I notice a small plume of black smoke coming up from down there.

Now I see what happened. Some fool managed to run off the straight road, just missing the bridge, and land upside down in the creek. The car—it looks like a Plymouth Barracuda—rolled as it skidded down the steep embankment, making a path through the kudzu and pine saplings. I smell broken earth and foliage along with the oily smoke.

The flames, mostly around the engine compartment, seem lazy—fed, I figure, by oil trickling out of the engine—but they're starting to spread. Me and Johnny are winded from running. Over the roaring in my ears, I pick up snatches of conversation. One guy with a gray flattop and a cigar in his mouth says, "Yeah, damn hippie. Got out and ran off through the woods. Probably carrying drugs."

One of the troopers asks, "Did you see the driver get out?"

"Well, no. But that guy over there said he did."

Another trooper is leaning against his car yapping on the radio. All around us people are talking, shouting, pointing, and the flashing lights are going like crazy.

One trooper tells another, "We've got to clear the highway. Fire truck's on the way."

Johnny looks at me, raises his eyebrows.

Then we see Eddie Lafitte running into the scene from the opposite direction. Eddie's a tough son-of-a-bitch. Used to be varsity fullback when we were in eighth grade. He's running stiff-legged with a knee that won't bend. He came home from Nam a while back with a Purple Heart.

Eddie pushes his way through the crowd and looks down the embankment. "Anybody in the car?" he asks the crowd in general. Several shrug their shoulders. The guy with the cigar looks away. A fat woman holding a child says, "I don't think nobody knows for sure."

Eddie throws his arms up. "The damn car's on fire and nobody knows if there's anybody in it?"

This gets the attention of the deputy. "Sir. We need you to calm down. The fire department is on their way. We'll dowse those flames, then we can get close enough to inspect—"

Eddie shouts back, "I don't see no truck coming. There could be people dying in there." Then, before the deputy or anybody else has time to react, Eddie's over the guard rail, sliding down the embankment, his stiff leg acting as a brake.

The deputy shouts, "Damn! You get back up here. That gas tank could blow any minute."

The bank gets really steep near the creek. By the time he's able to stop himself, Eddie's almost on top of the burning car. Then he's beside it in the creek, water not quite up to his knees. He squats down into the water and mud, trying to see inside the car. He starts yelling. "He's in there, dammit. There's a man in there!" The front of the car is engulfed now, and I figure the person Eddie sees must be baking.

Eddie tries to reach the door handle, but it's too hot. He starts slinging handfuls of water and mud onto the car. "Throw me a bucket," he yells. "Somebody throw me a damn bucket!"

A red-faced man with knobby elbows produces a five-gallon plastic bucket from his pickup. "Here, use this." He tosses the bucket over the rail. It bounces and flips end over end, lands on the other side of the creek. Eddie slogs and crawls for it, grabs the handle, starts dipping and slinging water at the burning car. He's gone primitive down there with his stiff leg, wrestling against the current and the weight of the bucket as he tries to reach the flames with water.

The fire truck's coming now, siren blaring and lights flashing, but traffic is still backed up. A trooper waves cars through. Others are parked in the fire truck's way. It takes a long time to get the truck into position and the hoses ready. Eddie keeps fighting the flames with his bucket. Me and Johnny, along with everybody else, watch him slipping and falling, wearing himself out.

Finally the pumper's ready. Water gushes from the hose over the edge. Eddie gets soaked and falls a few more times before he can get back up the bank. I lose track of him when I see a new set of flashing lights coming down the highway, a wrecker. The firemen keep pumping water over the bank. The stubborn flames finally die. More time passes as firemen, troopers, and the wrecker people talk about what to do next. They want to be sure there's no danger of that gas tank blowing while they're down there trying to hook the cable.

Johnny elbows me. "Where's Eddie?"

"I don't know." We look through the spectators and up and down the highway.

A guy with rubber boots and heavy gloves finally starts down the embankment with the cable unwinding from the wrecker. Men talk in guttural grunts. Eddie's gone.

The burnt Barracuda slowly rises from the mud, dragged on its top through vines and broken saplings. The crowd, quiet now, gathers to see what's inside.

Some turn away as the dead man starts to show through the driver's side window. I hear gasps and moans, exclamations of "Oh my God!"

His hands are talons clawing at the crazed window glass, and his face—or what's left of it—is pressed against it. His teeth seem huge in his wide, lipless mouth.

Firemen and ambulance workers pry the door open and lift out the burnt carcass, wet and gooey, with a cracked layer of black char over oozing pink meat. One of the ambulance guys brings a body bag.

I turn to Johnny. "Let's go."

We don't talk on the way to the car. After we're rolling down the highway, Johnny says, "I guess barbecue's out of the picture now."

"Yep. Definitely out."

"What then?"

"Get a six-pack, I guess."

"We gotta clock in after while."

"So?"

We get some beer and start guzzling. We ride over familiar back roads with Johnny's foot light on the pedal. After a while the beer starts sloshing inside my empty stomach as we wait for our shift to begin. Wondering about Eddie and why he took off like he did, I see the burnt man's death grimace. From where we were we didn't hear the screams, but poor Eddie—he was right there.

SPOOKY HOUSE

I NEVER WANTED TO GO inside that old farmhouse with crime tape around it and the gaping hole in the roof. I knew what had happened there and had been trying to forget it before I met Jack. The story though, when I reluctantly told it, heightened his desire to explore inside. Now, the house looms in my mind, along with images of what happened.

Jack loved rummaging through old barns and abandoned shacks just to see what he could find, and the rural road we traveled provided many opportunities. I'll admit it was fun, the feeling of intruding on another life, even though that other life had long since departed, and sometimes we did find stuff—knives, old books, bottles, antique car parts, rusty tools—random, cast-off items that were not quite worthless. We didn't think of it as stealing. Jack rationalized, saying, "Nobody wants this junk. It's just sitting here wasting. We can find some use for it." Honestly, he was always looking for that rare find, some valuable relic he could sell for a bundle on eBay. I went along for the ride, except when he got interested in that particular house. I objected and tried to resist but couldn't.

We passed it on the way to our afternoon and Saturday job at the big fireworks store just over the state line. Getting there from campus took thirty minutes over curvy back roads. It was too far to go for college students working part-time, but the money was good, and the work easy, much better than the last job I'd gotten fired from, tossing pizza and serving beer at Gianni's Place near the campus in Aaronville. Finding a decent job can be tough for a college guy, especially one with a natural aversion to work.

Getting on at Crazy Bob's Fireworks had been easy because Crazy Bob is my uncle. I grew up in a fireworks family. My father helped start the business with Uncle Bob when I was a kid, right after the interstate opened up through Okatchee, our one-traffic-light town. Jack thought the whole fireworks thing was really interesting. "What do you do in a fireworks store, besides sit around and wait for the Fourth of July and New Year's Eve?" he asked. "How did your family ever get into such a business? How did they make the *connections*? I mean, is there like a directory of wholesale fireworks suppliers or an association of distributors? Did your dad and uncle attend a marketing seminar? Go to conventions in Vegas every year?"

I explained that it's like any other business. We sold products at a profit, striving for volume, and location was everything. We were situated off the interstate ramp, just inside the state line that separated legal sales from forbidden fruit. Jack thought the idea of his becoming a roommate with a guy whose uncle Bob sold fireworks seemed "improbable." When I told him we could both get jobs there, that he could see firsthand what you do in a fireworks store, he laughed. "How random is that! Sure, I'd love to work at Crazy Bob's." He smiled, looking at something in the distance, probably already imagining how he would update his Facebook profile.

Jack is pretty cool, I'll admit. He came to Aaron-Maslow on a baseball scholarship. And he looks like the frat boy type with his thick, sandy hair, athletic build, and Abercrombie and Fitch clothes. But he's not. Which explains how I met him and how we got to be roommates. I'd decided by the beginning of fall semester to get away from Okatchee and my parents' house. Mom and Dad were happy for me to stay at home and commute to classes each day, but I'd realized I was missing out on some important aspects of college life, namely being able to drink and party all night. I discovered an old house for rent off campus that was cheaper than the dorms, especially with a roommate to share expenses. I put up a few notices on the bulletin boards and an ad in the college paper.

When Jack called, he suggested we meet at Suds and Silk at four in the afternoon, happy hour. This place was an old Victorian house near campus that had been converted into a restaurant and sports bar. I got there first and took a booth in the corner across from the big flatscreen mounted on the wall. The sports announcers were in their fancy studio giving rundowns and showing clips from the week's contests, highlighting a championship ultimate fighting match. They replayed the clip at least three times of the loser getting kicked in the head and collapsing in a heap. The other guy jumped on top of him and punched him twice more in his face before the referees pulled him off. I was thinking about what a rough sport that was and how crazy those guys must be when Jack walked in.

We shook hands and said, "Glad to meet you." Then, as soon as he settled into the booth, Jack ordered a pitcher of draft. He seemed incredibly thirsty, drinking about half of his sloppily poured mug in a gulp. Then he started asking a bunch of questions. He didn't know much about the area, this being his first semester. He found it fascinating that

I was from a nearby small town, just across the state line, and he wanted to know what it was like growing up in such a rural place. He was from an Atlanta suburb and had attended a high school with about two thousand students. He told me about his baseball team going to State, and how the scouts had recruited him, but it wasn't like he was bragging. He talked about himself in an offhand way and seemed more interested in my life and what we did for entertainment "out in the country."

"Where is the nearest mall?" he asked.

"Thirty or forty miles," I answered, "either east or west, toward Atlanta or Birmingham. Take your pick."

This seemed hard for him to grasp. He'd grown up practically in the middle of shopping malls and skate parks, pizza places with arcades, multi-plex theaters. He shook his head and began to look around the bar, like he was trying to figure out a riddle. I decided it would be a good time to tell him about cow tipping, how it was a favorite pastime among my old high school buddies. This was a lie of course, cow tipping being more rural myth than an actual thing, but I figured it would play well with this guy who'd probably never been around a real cow.

He answered, "Yeah, right. I've already tried cow-tipping. Cows sleep lying down. If they're standing there and two or three guys walk toward them, they just move away. Whole thing's a myth. You're gonna have to do better than that."

Impressive. I conceded that we didn't really tip cows, but we did spend lots of time drinking beer and riding around the back roads, which we had plenty of. "Within a few minutes," I said, "I could have you so far out in the sticks, you'd hear banjos playing, like in that old movie *Deliverance*."

"Cool. Let's do it."

"Now?"

"Not right this minute. We've got a pitcher of beer to finish. Then we'll need to look at that house you're interested in renting."

So, that's how it got started. We decided talking to a potential landlord after drinking so much beer would not be a good idea and spent the evening instead cruising through some of the rural areas surrounding Aaronville and the campus. I took him out Hog Liver Road toward the state line, a winding route that provides a shortcut to the interstate, one exit before Crazy Bob's. It also passes by that damned house that I wish had been bulldozed.

With our bellies full of beer, we'd both become lethargic, but Jack leaned forward and craned his neck as we passed. "Wow!" he said, noticing the black hole in the roof from the fire and the yellow tape still hanging limply around the front porch. "What happened there?"

Several months had passed since the tragedy, but the story was still fresh in my mind. It was the kind of thing that stayed with you, especially since it happened so near to where I'd grown up. I even knew the victims and the perpetrators.

Four old people, the Bledsoe family, had lived together in that farmhouse for years, ever since the brothers, who had never married, were born. The brothers were in their fifties, and Mr. and Mrs. Bledsoe … well, who knew how old they were? They were farm people in the old-fashioned sense, loved and respected in the community. They raised all sorts of animals—everything from goats and pigs to exotic roosters, turkeys, and guinea fowl. They kept bees and sold honey. They also sold vegetables every summer from a large, well-tended garden, and they usually ran thirty or forty head of cattle inside their fenced, rolling pastures.

They possessed skills that most everyone had either forgotten or never learned. The old man was one of the few left in the area who could re-cane porch rockers with strips he cut from white oak and ash trees. I remember when I was a kid my mom taking him a chair to fix and being amazed at the time he was willing to spend on such a tedious task. It must have taken him the better part of a week to re-weave that old rocker, and he only charged Mom ten bucks. When she pressed a few extra dollars on him, he insisted that we take a jar of honey back with us.

The brothers, Ned and Willard, had skills of their own. When they were young, they got interested in Volkswagens and turned one of the old barns into a repair shop. For about a decade they produced all sorts of souped-up Beetles and dune buggies. They were still taking on the occasional restoration project up until a year or two ago. I remember many times riding by the house with Mom or Dad and seeing a fixed-up Beetle, shining like brand new, sitting under the oak tree in the front yard with a For Sale sign in the window. They also restored old John Deere tractors, the ancient, two-cylinder kind that made the *thump-thump* exhaust sound.

And motorcycles too. Willard, the younger brother, became a British bike enthusiast, of all things. According to the stories I grew up hearing, he always had a need for more speed than they could get from those old Volkswagens, even the souped-up ones, and he was famous for ripping up and down the winding roads on his Norton 750 Commando. Their collection over the years of motorcycles, VWs, tractors, and parts had accumulated to the point of filling up a couple of old barns and a chicken house on the lower side of the property behind the steep-roofed farmhouse that in those days looked pristine. The structures were visible from the road, and the area residents often speculated about what they contained.

Everyone thought the Bledsoes were rich, that besides the treasure concealed within the barns and outbuildings they had cash stashed inside that old house, up in the attic maybe or buried under the back porch. And, like most places, Okatchee and the surrounding area contained its share of derelicts, drunks, and dope heads. Crimes that had in previous years been unheard of had been on the increase lately—thefts, burglaries, even a couple of rape cases—and meth labs were springing up everywhere. A countywide drug task force had been initiated, and the sheriff's department had added a cruiser and a couple of deputies.

My parents and most of the older folks blamed the Mexicans. There had been quite an influx, attributable to the interstate that ran right through the middle of the county. The Okatchee High student population had grown considerably in recent years, and special teachers had been hired to help the Hispanic students learn English. There had been several Mexican kids in my graduating class. One of them, Hector, was involved in the crime. He wasn't the instigator, though. I knew him from school as a quiet follower, a bit surly, but not the type to plan and carry out something like that. I blame it mostly on that other dude, Edward, who had also been in my class but dropped out in tenth grade.

Edward had always been bad, someone who would take advantage of weaker kids to get what he wanted or just for the fun of it. Back in sixth grade he kept picking on this nerdy kid named Reese who was always carrying around Manga books and Yu-Gi-Oh cards. Reese advertised his fantasy world with a vinyl lunchbox plastered with pictures of characters from the "Shadow Realm." He was an easy target.

Reese got sick of having his precious cards snatched away from him and sailed across the recess yard, and he got tired of having his peanut butter sandwiches and Oreos stolen from that Shadow Realm box. He tried to fight back one day, unfortunately for him, on the backside of the monkey bars, out of sight of Ms. Renfro. Edward made great sport of holding the chubby boy down, twisting his neck to make him squeal. Reese bucked and thrashed trying to get Edward off, but soon weakened, lapsing into sobs and minor convulsions. Edward, keeping Reese's arms pinned with his shins, slid down so that his crotch was in the weaker boy's face. He pressed himself against him, making sexual motions, and laughed in a raspy, hissing voice. "Squeal like a pig," he said. "Squeal like a pig." It was disgusting.

I stood and watched, along with several other kids. I wanted to help Reese, but Edward, who had been held back a couple of grades, was bigger and stronger. I was afraid. I didn't want to end up getting Edward's crotch in my face. So I stood there, trying to muster the courage to do something. I tried to at least look away, to not provide an audience and contribute to Reese's humiliation, but I couldn't even do that. Finally, this lanky girl saw what was happening and ran to get Ms. Renfro. Somebody warned Edward, so there wasn't much for the teacher to see by the time she got there. None of us—not even Reese—would corroborate the girl's story, so Edward got away with his cruelty as usual. I realize now that this became a pattern in his life that I had contributed to through my weakness. But, what the hell, we can't all be heroes.

I don't know how Edward got involved with the Bledsoe brothers. The newspapers made it sound like he and Hector targeted them, looking for easy drug money. A rumor went around the community, though, that there was more to it than that. Neighbors had seen Edward's beat-up Camaro in the driveway and him and Hector coming out of the house on several occasions, weeks before the actual crime. Some thought that Willard and Ned had hired the boys to help put up a sawmill on the back side of the property; others thought there was something else going on.

That part of the story never made it into the newspapers. The accounts only focused on how Edward and Hector were captured minutes after leaving the scene of the crime and how the bank teller had tipped off the sheriff's department that something wasn't right after Ned had pulled into the drive-thru looking distressed—with Edward in the truck with him—wanting to withdraw ten-thousand dollars. She made up some excuse about the computers being down and said he would have to come back later. By the time the sheriff got around to checking on the Bledsoes, the fire department had already doused the flames.

The charred, soaked bodies were found piled on top of each other in the back room where the fire had been started. The investigators found a blackened baseball bat, and each of the four Bledsoes had a cracked skull. The newspaper also reported that the house had been ransacked and that Edward and Hector had large sums of cash in their possession when they were captured.

That was about it, all any of us knew anyway. The last newspaper story reported, "The suspects were charged with felony murder and ordered to be held without bond." The flurry of gossip died down. It seemed that nobody wanted to talk about what had happened to the Bledsoes, but the partially burned farmhouse stood as a reminder to everyone who traveled that country road—including Jack and me, every afternoon on our way to Crazy Bob's Fireworks.

It was a dry autumn, so the leaves bypassed yellow and red, going straight to brown as they turned and fell. Jack, curious about everything, suggested our first explorations. We started poking around in the abandoned barns and farmhouses on our way to work, pulling his Civic or my Ranger over and parking just far enough down a logging road or behind a shed to be out of sight of the light passing traffic. We never saw anybody. He often wondered where the people were who owned the old places. "I don't know," I would answer. "I guess they either died off or moved away to the city."

One old house, only a few miles from the Bledsoe place, was particularly interesting. This one had a faded For Sale sign in front, which made Jack even bolder. "If anyone asks what we're doing," he said, "we can act like we're interested in buying the place." Yeah, right, I thought. We look like a couple of real estate tycoons.

It was a small frame house with peeling paint and a flimsy metal carport to one side. The yard and shrubs had been untended for some time. I noticed a dented metal dog food bowl next to the concrete steps that led to the front porch, and a garden hose lay coiled in a tangle of brown weeds at the corner of the house.

There were three small rectangular windows in the front door, arranged in a stair-step pattern. Jack peered through the middle one. "Wow. There's all sorts of stuff in there." He placed his hand on the knob and turned. "Come on," he said. "It's open."

I held back. "I dunno. What if the owners come up, or the sheriff?" But he was already inside. Not wanting to stand around on the porch or wait in the car, I followed.

The place had that smell old people's houses sometimes get, the shut-up smell of space heaters, cats, and snuff. And

Jack was right. There was junk everywhere, most of it piled in various heaps in the floor: blankets, quilts, dresses, books, boxes of dishes, and framed photographs of people in big-collared shirts and leisure suits standing in front of old cars smoking cigarettes. It looked like someone—maybe family members or the real estate people—had started cleaning out the place but got disgusted and quit.

The rooms were small with sticky linoleum on the floor, except for the first one we entered, which had this filthy orange carpet that looked like it had been there since the seventies. The walls were paneled with flimsy, fake woodgrain.

I was moving slowly through the debris when Jack called out from the kitchen, "Hey man, you've got to see this!"

When I got there he turned from the counter to face me, holding a big-ass meat cleaver, like something from a George Romero movie. "I'm keeping this," he said.

It took me a second to recover from the creepy thoughts that popped into my brain. The kitchen smelled rancid and I noticed several dead roaches on the floor and counter tops. "Why?" I finally asked.

"For one thing, I like the way it feels in my hand, and, who knows, we may need it to defend ourselves against burglars—or *zombies*."

"I thought that's what the baseball bat beside your bed was for."

"True. The bat is my preferred first line of defense, but I'm sure we could find a use for this fine utensil. Come here and hold it. Just feel how heavy it is."

"Yeah, great. I'll take your word for it. Let's get out of here. This place stinks."

We finally left after Jack had gone through the kitchen drawers and the bedroom closets. He got excited over an old eight-track tape deck and was going to take it, but left it behind when he discovered half of its guts were hanging out. That meat cleaver, though, he was proud of that thing—still has it, I guess—but I really don't know what he did with it.

At any rate, it whetted his appetite for formerly occupied space to poke around in. His desire was with us each day, hanging like fog inside the vehicle, as we rode by the Bledsoe's old farmhouse. I felt it more when I was driving and he was free to look at things. A week or so after the meat cleaver house Jack said, "We've got to do it. We've got to go in that house where those old people got killed."

"Hell no," I said. "I ain't going in there. That place is creepy."

I glanced over and saw that he was smiling at me, his opaque eyes reflecting an odd light.

So, I gave in and that's how I came to be in this condition. The inside of that damned house has become the most vivid of my memories, and the weirdest part is now I see things in my mind that I didn't even see that day. We did it a couple of weeks before Christmas break, went inside that place where horrible deaths had occurred. I followed Jack's suggestion and parked my truck behind the house. Together we mounted the part of the back porch that wasn't burned.

God, I don't want to describe it, but I can't help thinking about it. The dreams are the worst part. I wake up sometimes thinking I'm there as it's happening. I hear the bat cracking against skulls, the shrieks, curses, grunts, and moans. It usually takes a few minutes to shake it off, to convince myself that it was a dream. When this happens, I feel blood pulsing in my temples and eyes. It takes effort to separate the real sounds from the sounds in my mind, but eventually, I'll hear Jack's snoring and rhythmic breathing as he sleeps, untroubled by nightmares. Then I know where I am, but the night is ruined, all hope of sleep lost.

Everything is suffering now. During the day, when I'm sitting in class trying to concentrate, pictures flash behind my eyelids each time I blink, and I don't mean spring break images of hot chicks in thongs like normal college guys fantasize about. No, I see images of charred baseball bats, *even though I didn't actually see such a thing.* The baseball bat wasn't there. The police had taken it away as evidence. I wonder, though, where they found it. Part of the floor in that room was burned through. Had the murder weapon fallen to the ground where the hounds slept underneath the house?

The newspaper account didn't provide those kinds of details, the things I really wanted to know. It only said, "The suspected murder weapon, a baseball bat partially burned from the fire, was discovered and collected at the scene along with other evidence." How can people write shit like that? That's another thing that's ruined for me. I was planning to go into journalism next semester and had even talked to the people in the office about getting on the newspaper staff. Now I can't imagine interviewing people—adults, professors, deans, committee chairmen— about things like the building plans for new dormitories or the renovation of the old auditorium. Who cares about that sort of thing? How can you write about the mundane things of life when you're tortured by things you've seen and haven't seen?

I see Jack in my dreams now, and Edward. Sometimes Jack is Edward and vice-versa. Edward and Hector holding the Bledsoe brothers down, making them squeal like pigs. Jack, heavy and strong, holding me down, his crotch in my face. Sometimes he has that meat cleaver. And those magazine images keep coming back.

There was a stack of them in one of the bedroom closets. The roof over most of the house was intact, so everything was preserved just as it had been that day, the day of the crime. The stuff of their lives was dumped out everywhere: shoeboxes filled with cancelled checks, keychains, pocketbooks, pocket knives, horse-show trophies, catalogs, walking sticks, the old woman's walker, medicine bottles, moldy encyclopedias, flashlight batteries, alarm clocks, raincoats … you get the picture. The worst part, though, was that closet. Their clothes were still hanging in there!

Those shirts, overalls, jackets, and boots got Jack really excited. He was deep into the back of the narrow space when he shouted out, "No way! You've got to see this!" I felt sick but was compelled to look nevertheless. Jack was coming out of the closet, laughing, waving the thing in his hand. He threw it at me, almost in my face. I caught it and immediately noticed the lurid title and picture on the front. The magazine was titled *Thrust*, and it was filled with photos of naked men engaged in all sorts of bizarre sex acts.

"Sick!" I said, tossing it aside.

Jack grinned. "Looks like there was some kinky shit going on here at the old Bledsoe place. There's a whole pile of 'em in the back of the closet."

I stood in the middle of the room not knowing what to do or where to look. I was standing between twin beds, the frames at least; the mattresses and bedclothes were dumped onto the floor. The room was arranged with a bed and chest of drawers on each side and the shared closet, where Jack was having so much fun, on one end. The furnishings looked like they were from the fifties. Thinking about Ned and Willard living in this same arrangement since they were kids made my knees weak. My guts felt like they were boiling.

Jack had completely disappeared inside the closet. I called out to him, "Hey man, let's go. This place is making me sick."

A muffled voice answered: "Sure, I'm ready when you are." Then he stepped out.

I stood blinking at what I saw. Jack was leaning against the door wearing a black leather jacket that must have been left over from Willard's motorcycle days. It looked like part of James Dean's wardrobe. The room began to spin as Jack held that pose. I remember him saying, "It's a perfect fit. I think I'll keep it." The pile of stuff in the floor was sucking me downward and there was a rushing sound in my ears. After that my mind skips. I don't remember leaving the house, but I do remember yelling, "Oh hell no! Take that damn thing off."

But I don't think he did. In the dream he still has it on. There's this recurring part where he's grinning and saying, "Come on, let's do it," as he holds open the passenger door of a bathtub Porsche like James Dean's. "Oh hell no! Oh hell no!" I say over and over.

I don't believe in ghosts. Nothing happened that doesn't happen in a normal world. We went back to our little house in town, back to our jobs at Crazy Bob's, back to classes, but none of it works anymore. Nothing seems real now.

I'm looking for a way to make things right. Surely there are others who suffer like me, who've had their worlds turned inside out. I need rest and medication to help me function. At night when I'm trying to sleep, drifting in and out as Jack snores beside me, I can see his bat through the grain of darkness, leaning against the wall beside the bed. I hate his erratic, raspy snoring, the fact that he can sleep and I can't. I partially rise, then shake my head to dislodge the frightening thoughts. I know medicine will help, it just has to. I cling to the belief that soon, with the right prescription, I'll be okay.

THE BOILER ROOM

I KNEW BRETT WELL, having been his teacher before his life began to deteriorate. I'd seen his dark moods grow darker, and I'd also experienced those occasional moments when he could look around the low-vaulted basement and make himself believe it was only temporary, not so bad after all. It really wasn't. We both loved the smell and the antiquity, an ambience born of piping, gauges, valves, and the massive black iron of the old boiler that hadn't been used for years. A beat-up teacher's desk and rolling chair occupied one corner. On top of the desk sat a cast-off computer, too slow for the teachers but good enough for the janitorial department. Cleaning supplies, mop buckets, and floor buffing equipment were neatly arranged along the opposite wall. As "acting" lead-man on the evening shift crew at Whitefield High School, Brett felt better when things were organized. The boiler room served as his headquarters every weekday from four in the afternoon until midnight. I visited him there whenever I could.

Coach Puckett had helped procure the job for him and engineered his quick promotion. Coach pretended to still believe in him and stopped by most afternoons to chat and offer encouragement. "How's the therapy going," he'd ask. "You still doing those stretches and bends?" During the fall Coach had arranged things so Brett could leave his janitorial duties for a couple of hours to help out at the practice field, working with the linebackers. But now it was winter, and he reported directly to the boiler room each day at four or a few minutes early to go over the schedule and to be sure the supply inventory was up to date.

~

DETAILS FRESH IN HIS MIND of his triumphant senior year—the state championship, scholarship offers, accolades, willing girls—had provided encouragement during the first round of disasters when his father walked out on him and his mother to marry a younger woman. The supper-table announcement a week after his eighteenth birthday had been a slap to Brett's face, a knockout punch to his mom.

"I have a life too," his father had said. "When I'm with Stephanie … well, it's hard to explain. Things click. We get each other. It's time now for me to realize my dreams, and they include her. Brett has his future laid out for him. We've done a good job, but, honey, you know how it is between us. There's really not much anymore, besides Brett, I mean. I feel I should set you free to live your life, so you'll have a chance to find someone who'll love you the way you deserve to be loved." There was a catch in his voice and he blinked his wet eyes before looking into his plate.

Brett's mother glanced upward then brought her gaze down to the top of her husband's head as if to see through the bald spot and into his brain.

He looked up. "We'll get through this."

She slid back her chair, rose from the table, and walked calmly into the kitchen, where she started breaking things. The racket of china hitting the floor, silverware ringing against the wall, banging pots and pans, and her screeching and cursing was like nothing Brett had ever heard. The realization came slowly that this was real, and by the time he reached her she had collapsed onto the floor, sobbing, ruined, along with the broken dishes, dumped-out pot roast, and strewn squash casserole.

He knelt and placed his arm around her trembling shoulders. "Mom. No. Mom."

She raised her head, and Brett turned to see his father standing over them, his hands in erasing motion, indicating that they'd somehow misunderstood a simple math problem. "No. It doesn't—"

"This is me!" she screamed, a sweeping gesture indicating the wreckage around her.

"That's just how it seems now. With time you'll see. This will be better for all of us."

She grabbed a plate fragment and threw it at him. "Get out! Get out!"

With a look on his face combining pity and disgust, he turned and left them alone.

Brett helped his mom up and into the bathroom. She leaned heavily against him, taking in quick breaths and exhaling little sobs. She closed the door, and he stood for a while in the hallway, his mind a glitchy PC struggling to reboot.

Over the next few weeks he withdrew as much as possible from all events involving his parents, taking refuge with friends, or losing himself in video games and social media. He had much to think about: his final days of high school, graduation, and enjoying a short break before reporting to summer workouts at the University of West Alabama. So much happening so fast made him dizzy, but there was also the liberating sense of starting a new life and leaving the past behind. His parents' troubles, unless he slowed down long enough to consider them, were smudged background pieces, bringing his exciting new life into sharper relief.

～

BRETT AND ROSEMARY had been breaking up and getting back together since their sophomore year. She was a willowy girl with straw-colored hair, freckles across her nose, and mischievous green eyes. They'd sat next to each other in math class. Brett was good at math; Rosemary was not, and often needed help. They laughed at her ineptitude while the teacher, Ms. Duvall, winked at their developing relationship. Soon they were "talking," sending flirtatious text messages. Within a few weeks they were officially "going out." The thrill of losing their innocence and exploring new sexual frontiers was intense but short lived, at least for Brett. As a sophomore he was already a starting varsity player. By his junior year he was sacking quarterbacks and averaging ten tackles per game. A defensive player on the field, off field he scored at will inside his growing female fan base.

Brett and Rosemary's changing relationship was rife with drama and became the stuff of countless Facebook posts and Twitter insults. Friends took sides. They all became characters in each other's soap operas, and meaningful classroom instruction became increasingly difficult for us teachers. I continued to prepare challenging lessons and present them in as lively a manner as I could, but I felt myself being drawn into their world, realizing it was real while the one I offered was not. Their lives and impulses were immediate, involving friends and hormones. Most of what I taught was ancient history. My lessons over the Puritan influence, the Revolution, Romanticism, and the other movements produced yawns while Rosemary's posts about Brett's little cock, although not true, generated laughter throughout the school and a catalog of posted comments.

The fact that they didn't end up hating each other but kept coming back together after multiple encounters with others was a testament to their mutual attraction and the imprinting effect of first-time sex. And Brett's mom loved Rosemary, especially after Brett's dad left. One evening a week or so after graduation she said, "Let's the three of us have dinner together tonight. You can light the grill, and I'll make those spicy burgers y'all like. I love to watch that girl eat. To be so skinny, she's really got an appetite. She hasn't been over in a while. Why don't you call her? It'll be fun. And you can go by Redbox and pick out a movie."

"Mom," Brett said, "You know Rosemary and me broke up. We're both seeing other people now."

His mother sighed. "Well, you can always get back together. I believe some people are meant for each other. It's a chemistry thing, something your father and I apparently lacked. Are you still talking to her at least?"

"Yes, Mom. We're friends now."

"You know you like her better than those other girls."

That much was true, so Brett on that evening relented. They ate burgers, potato salad, and homemade onion rings. Mom even provided them with beer while she enjoyed a few glasses of wine on the couch as they watched some stupid action flick, her husband's recliner sitting empty on the other side of the room.

~

THAT SUMMER WAS TRAUMATIC in many ways. As if his father's abrupt departure, his mother's subsequent meltdown, and the frenetic pace of his changing circumstances weren't enough, what Brett faced on the university campus, after the shortest summer break of his life, became another battering force. In high school he had been one of the biggest, strongest, fastest guys on the team. Here he was barely average, below average in fact, considering the returning players were already two weeks into the program when he and the other newcomers arrived.

From the first day he was dizzied by the geography of an unfamiliar place along with complicated workout and class schedules. Just getting to where he was supposed to be—dorm, weight room, practice field, dining hall, and classrooms on the other side of campus—had presented an unprecedented challenge. His confusion amplified his embarrassment at not being able to perform as many reps with as much weight or keep up during agility drills. By the third day there was much soreness but little improvement, and he was still prone to starting out across the quad toward the dining hall when he'd meant to go to the practice field.

Brett told himself over and over that he could do this, but the self-talk wasn't convincing, especially when the returning players taunted him. A big lineman from Birmingham looked him up and down and said, "Dude, did you guys even have a weight program at that little hick high school you came from? Because, like, I'm just not seeing the results. Besides strength deficits, your technique totally sucks."

"Sure. We had an awesome weight program. Coach Puckett pushed us hard. I just didn't do much over the off-season. A little out of practice. I'll catch up with you guys soon enough."

I've seen Brett's determined side, so I know he was trying his hardest. But sometimes determination isn't enough when you're up against so many unseen forces. In high school the nascent enemy camp was outmatched by Brett's forward momentum as part of a championship team, even though by then his faith must have been wavering. The football season and the demands of his social life had taken their toll, and his grades were declining. After I'd informed Coach Puckett and his parents that without high marks on the paper and the final exam he would fail my class, Brett showed up for after-school tutoring. I looked up from my paper grading on the Friday afternoon before exam week, only days away from Christmas break, to find him standing in front of my desk.

He cleared his throat. "Mr. Stiles. I think I need help."

I answered, "Yes, Brett, I think you do too."

He stood there, hands at his sides, eyes shifting about. He was dressed for high school success in his Hollister shirt and Abecrombie jeans, but he exuded an aura of failure. This was the first time I'd felt it.

"What are you stuck on?" I said. "Which topic did you choose? You do have a topic?"

He looked at the floor, then at the corner of my desk. "That's just it. I was gonna do something about that Thoreau guy, "the Walden experiment," but I couldn't find much. So I switched to "the origins of American Romanticism," but that's just too hard. Every time I type something into Google I get a bunch of stuff that doesn't make sense. I don't even know what I'm doing or how to get started."

"So you've got nothing." I resisted the impulse to lecture him about how he'd be finished by now if he'd paid attention and followed the prescribed steps when I presented the videos over the research process. I wanted to remind him of all the times I'd caught him texting, sleeping, or on inappropriate websites, but I didn't. I did, though, let out an audible sigh as I pushed papers out of the way. "Okay.

Grab a chair and come around here. Let's go over that list of topics."

I got him hooked on "the death of Edgar Allan Poe," and sat with him at a computer until he had several good sources and a preliminary thesis. We worked as the cleaning crew ran their floor buffers up and down the hall, and it was nearly six p.m. before we left my room. He had a good start now, and he promised he'd have the paper finished by the following Monday. I wasn't surprised when he proudly handed in his work the first thing that morning, nor was I surprised by the quality. It wasn't an A paper—some passages were too closely paraphrased and would have been considered plagiarism earlier in the semester when I had been in strict, technical mode—but it was documented and formatted correctly, and it supported a logical thesis, that Poe had suffered and eventually died from a brain tumor. Brett would pass my class. In fact, he ended up with a low B after pulling a ninety-four on the final out of his ass. I was pleased that his GPA was safe, and I felt as though I'd made a difference.

～

THE INJURY THAT SENT BRETT HOME from the University of West Alabama and into the boiler room happened during the third week of summer conditioning. By that time he'd made a little progress in strength training and had finally learned his way around campus, but he was still behind. He'd pushed himself harder than usual in the weight room the day before and had noticed twinges in his left knee and lower back while doing squats. He needed to rest his body, but the schedule and the expectations of others wouldn't allow it. Cones were set up on the field the next day for drills that involved full-speed directional changes. This was the first time they'd done this routine, and Brett wanted to show that he could at least keep up with the linemen. The idea was to go around the last cone and then to cut back sharply and sprint to the sideline. Something snapped when he made the turn, and he collapsed midfield, writhing in agony.

After he'd returned home, I ran into him on the Whitefield High School campus, where I was teaching summer school. He'd hobbled into the building on crutches, a brace on his knee. I recognized him from down the hall. "Brett! What happened?" As I approached he eased around to face me, wincing, bearing his weight on his right leg.

"Oh, hello, Mr. Stiles." He seemed slightly embarrassed. "I got a little injury. I'm trying to find Coach Puckett."

"I don't think he's here today. He's been preoccupied lately."

"Yeah. I heard about it. Then I saw the newspaper this morning."

Brett was referring to an emerging scandal involving former teammates that threatened to rip our community apart. An after-graduation party had gotten out of hand on the weekend before he left for Livingston, a party that he would ordinarily have attended. The circumstances that kept him away could now be seen as a lone stroke of luck in an otherwise dismal run that began as his senior year ended, when his father walked out on him and his mom.

"It's a terrible situation, unfortunate for the guys, all of us. And of course the girl."

"I still can't believe it. Jeffrey, Conner, and Dillon, of all people. It's a wonder I wasn't there. Maybe if I had been, I could've done something."

"I'm glad you weren't there." I paused to watch his response, a slight nod. "So, you got a minute? Why don't you come down to the room. Take a load off and tell me what happened. Looks like it must've hurt."

He crutched along beside me. Once inside, I shut the door, gave him my comfortable chair, and pulled up an old straight-back for myself.

"What do you think'll happen to them?" he asked. "It's really serious, isn't it?"

"It's very serious, Brett. If they're convicted, they'll go to prison."

"I don't believe they did it. They're not like that. I mean, they don't need to rape girls. It's like … well, you know how it is."

Yes, I thought, nodding in agreement. I do know how it is with you kids and hormones and steroids and drugs and alcohol and a culture that promotes instant gratification and sex as a recreational sport.

"They're popular guys, and the girls—they're kinda everywhere, you know? Probably wasn't like that back in your day, was it?"

"People have always been … *lustful*, Brett—guys and girls. But opportunities are more abundant for your generation. There's less restraint now, but more drama with cell phones and the internet. Everything's out there and nothing's off-limits, or at least it seems that way. But, unfortunately for your friends, some things are still off-limits."

"Yeah. But it was just a party. I don't see how—"

"The girl was hospitalized. Rumors are it was pretty bad. Did you know her?"

"No. She went to Valley High."

"I'm sure some of her friends were there. She'll have lawyers and witnesses and the guys will have their lawyers and witnesses. There'll be evidence to consider and the doctor's testimony. It will all play out and hopefully justice will be served."

Brett shifted his weight in the chair, straightened his injured leg. "I don't want to see my friends go to jail. Their lives will be ruined."

"They're already damaged, even if they're found not guilty. They'll have a hard time shaking this. The way it looks now … well, it doesn't look good. There's been talk of pictures. On their cellphones. Pictures of the girl, passed out, and what they did to her. You don't know anything about that do you?"

"No. I ain't seen no pictures."

"Brett, you're talking to your former English teacher here."

"Oh, sorry. I *haven't* seen *any* pictures."

"I appreciate the grammar, but the truth would be nice."

He looked at the floor, then away.

～

I BELIEVE BRETT, at least part of him, wanted to go back to the university and play football, but after our chat that day I was pretty sure he wouldn't, even though the sport was in his blood. His dad had played for Whitefield during a streak of winning seasons. He hadn't made it as a college player, but attending Auburn for one semester qualified him for exalted fan status. On his mother's side Brett's uncle, Troy, had been an all-state player who'd received many scholarship offers. He and I were in the same class, although not friends. He was a jock, and I was a band nerd. Troy was a sadistic bastard then; now he was just an out-of-shape fuck-up, nicknamed Falcon for his brief stint on one of Atlanta's practice teams after he dropped out of UGA.

After his short-lived NFL experience, he got married and divorced three or four times, became a druggie and a drunk, and had several run-ins with the law. When Brett came home from Livingston, Falcon decided to become part of his nephew's life.

Often when I'd stop by the boiler room after work to visit Brett, Falcon would already be there. Sometimes Coach Puckett would be there too, and they'd be reminiscing about the big games. Under these circumstances I seldom lingered more than a few minutes, about how long it would take for Falcon to start teasing me, picking up an old high school thread tied to one of many embarrassing moments.

One of his favorite subjects had always been the storage room incident that left permanent emotional scars, even though I've consistently denied the story that I was caught masturbating in the band room. I'd lagged behind that day because of a heartsickness that had suddenly gotten worse. I couldn't go out there on that hot afternoon with those stupid cymbals to practice the same routine over and over, not after what had just happened.

I'd been trying to date a girl during that period, Maggie Beam. As in all my experiences with females, I was struggling to get out of what kids refer to now as "the friend zone." I'd been screwing up my courage for weeks to let her know how I felt. In the hubbub preceding practice, I managed to get her off by herself in a corner of the band room amid legions of wobbly music stands. I took her hand, looked her in the eyes, and said something incredibly lame: "Maggie, you're beautiful and I need you."

She laughed. "You're so horny! You don't need me, you just need to jerk off." Then she yanked back her hand and spun away to rejoin her friends, knocking over some junk in the process. I watched them leave, pushing, shoving, and carrying their instruments through the double doors that opened onto the practice field. I experienced a moment of nausea, then the need for darkness and quiet. I found myself inside the storage room—a nest of tambourines, wood blocks, plastic recorders, stacks of sheet music, and the book bags of my band mates. I closed the door.

I can only attribute it to a perverted sense of irony, actually doing what Maggie had heartlessly suggested. Maggie's best friend, Sue McBrayer, told the truth about what she'd seen. She left practice early for a dental appointment and returned alone to retrieve her books. In my reverie, I failed to hear her approach. She flung the door open on me reclining against the wall with my pants around my ankles, stiff penis in hand. She watched for long seconds as I fumbled to cover up. With a smirk she grabbed her bag and shut the door, not even trying to suppress her giggle. I hoped she wouldn't tell, but of course she did. When guys like Falcon got hold of the story, my high school humiliation and social exile were made complete.

～

THE BOILER ROOM had been a hangout since back in the nineties when the Whitefield campus was declared "tobacco free." For faculty members who smoked, the spartan, fusty space became a de facto teacher's lounge. I'd been spending stolen moments for some time there before Brett made it his headquarters; with him in residence, the old iron of the place became even more magnetic. This increased pulling power resided in his weakness, an inability to see beyond the current circumstances of his ignominious return to high school to work as a janitor. I sensed he was almost strong, almost a man, almost complete, and I also recognized his pain. My nurturing instinct, grown numb from years of teaching, was awakened by the recognition of a kindred suffering spirit.

I would have spent more time there had it not been for Falcon's frequent presence. My pattern, established before he started showing up, was to push through the squeaking door around 4:15 and make my way down the inclined concrete walkway to unwind and chat with Brett, whose workday was just beginning. I was surprised the first time I found my old high school nemesis in that low-ceilinged space, reclining in a castoff rolling chair with his feet propped on the battered desk as if he was running the show.

Coach Puckett was seated to his right on a blue cafeteria chair with a wobbly leg. Brett sat on a five-gallon bucket of floor cleaner, his back against the wall. Falcon was smoking, flicking ashes into an empty nut can.

As I entered he said, "Hey, Bernie, come on in. We were just talking about academic stuff, how important it is for athletes to maintain their grades. I remember yours were top-notch. I always wondered if people like you even had to study. Weren't you in Beta Club every year?"

"I did study, quite a bit in fact. All of us in Beta Club studied, had to. Keeping an A average requires work."

"Right, right. Don't I know it. You Beta Club kids were an inspiration to all us dummies, especially you. You were the *master* Beta!"

He grinned, raised an eyebrow, and looked to Coach Puckett for approval. A gravelly guffaw erupted from Coach's throat before he checked himself. Brett smiled, looked at the floor.

I'd developed a thick skin against jabs like this, but it hurt to have Brett think of me as the pitiable nerd, the object of adolescent insults. "Well," I said, "After all these years I'm glad to see you still enjoy joking about things that never happened. I could probably make jokes too about things that never happened, like your career. Whatcha doing for a living these days, Troy? Still hauling scrap metal on that old beat-up truck? Watching your retirement account grow?"

This brought another chuckle from Coach Puckett and a grin from Brett. Falcon knew he couldn't match me at verbal sparring, but he managed to throw some bravado into a weak comeback. "Retirement? Hell, I'm already retired. I do exactly what I want. Unlike you, I don't take orders from lard-assed principals and women. I been my own boss for years. I'm an *entrepreneur*. And, in case you didn't know, there's big money in scrap metal these days."

"That's awesome. Soon you'll be able to save enough to buy a truck made in this century." I grabbed a bucket, slid it around to form a circle with the guys. After sticking a cigarette to my lips I pulled out my lighter. Two thumb-strokes produced a tiny flame that flickered and failed. "Damn. These cheap things don't last—"

"Think fast, dude," Falcon said. With a quick sidearm motion, he pitched his lighter at my face. I snatched it from the air with my left hand, nonchalantly lit my smoke, and tossed it back to the desktop. It bounced onto his lap.

He gave me the same look I'd seen in PE class years ago in those moments before he committed some sadistic act: elbowing me in the nose under the basketball goal, karate chopping my Adam's apple in the locker room, or snatching down the ladder from the press box roof after sending me up to retrieve a stray softball. The look melted quickly, and he turned to Brett. "You know, Bernie here has a point. Making good grades does take work, but the payoff is worth it. When you get back to that university, I'm gon' expect you to hit those books hard, be the first in our family to actually finish. With a degree you can get some cushy job with a matching 401k, then sit back and let your ass get broad and soft like Bernie's."

I surprised him again with my willingness to counter punch. "That's good advice from your uncle Troy, Brett. In fact, he's a living example of what not to do. While I weigh less now than I did in high school, his belly has tripled in size. Of course, I never was athletic like you guys, but I've always wondered about that, how the jocks go to flab after their glory days are over. I guess keeping in shape, like studying, takes discipline."

Coach Puckett cleared his throat, rocked back in the overburdened chair, and glanced down at his own spare tire. Brett remained silent.

Troy squared his shoulders. "I may have gained a few pounds, but I can still kick your meat-beating ass. So things haven't really changed."

"Guess not. You always were a dangerous dude." I took a slow drag, then, regarding my companions, rose off the bucket as Falcon studied me. I stepped over to the desk and ground my cigarette out in the nut can. "I'll catch you guys later. Got some papers to grade. Tomorrow's another day."

"Me too," said Coach. "Better get back down to the field. See if I can get a decent scrimmage out of these guys. Nobody pushes hard unless I'm there. Say Brett, I was thinking. You wanna help us out some? Work with those young linebackers?"

"Sure, Coach. That'd be awesome. Thanks!"

"We'll talk more about it later. Maybe you can start next week."

Coach and I made our way up to the main hallway, leaving Brett in the boiler room with his uncle.

～

SUMMER LINGERED before suddenly giving way to fall. Leaves turned and fell, Fridays flew by, and a disappointing football season ended as a blemish on Coach Puckett's otherwise impressive record. He'd been preoccupied with the cancerous scandal that threatened to engulf his program. The rape case had prompted an investigation into an alleged teen sex ring emanating from the Whitefield High football team. Cell phones had been confiscated and more charges were expected. Coach, harried on all fronts, withered like the leaves and became a bitter old man. I stopped seeing him in the boiler room. I don't know where he went to smoke, but I do know he'd been called to the police station for questioning on several occasions. And he was taking lots of sick days.

Brett was also questioned. I knew he had plenty of other problems—a failing car, too little money, and an absent, selfish dad—so I tried to avoid the topic. This issue, though, like rat droppings on white china, couldn't be ignored. He brought it up himself late one chilly evening as we smoked and drank coffee in the boiler room. "You remember that day in your classroom right after I'd hurt my knee and come home? When you asked me if I'd seen any pictures?

I was leaning back in the wobbly chair. "Yep. I remember your pitiful self, hobbling along on those crutches."

"I lied about the pictures. Not seeing them, I mean. And I lied to the police too. Now I wonder if I did the right thing." He was sitting behind the desk with a pencil in hand, doodling.

I leaned forward, planting the chair firmly. "You don't have anything on your phone, do you? That could get you in trouble?"

"No. When that stuff was going on, my smart phone had died and I was using a little cheap thing. But I saw some of the pictures. Lots of people were involved. Most of the guys weren't even on the football team. And the girls, most of them were … you know—"

"Unpopular?"

"Yeah, the guys were just using them for kicks." He laid the pencil down and looked at me for a second before taking a sip of coffee.

"Those girls are marked for life now. Don't you think they deserve some justice?"

"The police don't need anything from me. They already got enough."

"But still. You said you weren't sure you'd done the right thing. How will you feel later?"

He shrugged, looked away, picked up the pencil.

"I'm glad you weren't involved."

"I knew about it when it first got started, right after Rosemary and me broke up. A lot of shit was flying around, making me kinda sick. We were saying stuff about each other and she was acting like she hated me. I was afraid she might do something stupid just to spite me."

"Rosemary?" I said, "She's smarter than that."

He reached in his shirt pocket for a cigarette. "She can get pretty crazy sometimes. I was worried enough that when Mom suggested I invite her over to the house for burgers and a movie, I agreed. That was the weekend before I left for Livingston, the same weekend of that party. That's why we weren't there. We almost got back together that night. Would have, I guess, if I hadn't been going away. That was her excuse at least. She said she didn't think a long-distance relationship would work for us." He blew an elongated smoke ring that quickly broke apart.

"You're not long distance now."

His face changed and I caught a glimpse of the darkness I'd not yet fathomed.

"Yeah. Nothing stays the same, does it?"

He raised himself off his chair, looking older than his years. "I need to get outta here. I should be helping the crew. We gotta do the gym floor tonight and scrub the locker rooms."

"Sure. I understand. I don't want to keep you from your work."

"Come back later in the week."

I helped him load the supply cart and push it up the ramp. He passed through the door first, and I watched him roll his equipment down the hall, still walking with a slight limp that was noticeable to me if not others.

～

I DROPPED BY ON FRIDAY evening around eight o'clock, a new time I preferred since I was less likely to run into Falcon or anyone else at this hour. Brett usually arranged the schedule to allow for some quiet time in the boiler room while the crew went about their duties. I'd started using the back door, which Brett kept unlocked when he was expecting me. This forgotten entrance was accessible through a service road behind the cafeteria. When I saw Falcon's truck parked in the gravel, my first impulse was to drive by, but I had as much right to be there as he did. My emotions were tangled, but part of me wanted to offset Falcon's negative influence. I guess another part was a glutton for punishment.

The rusty back door rested behind a retaining wall, at the bottom of a narrow stairway. It opened into a low concrete corridor with black iron pipes filling the upper portion at head level. The pipes of the obsolete steam system bulged with valves and gauges whose only purpose now was to bruise unwary heads. They'd inflicted me with a few knots before I learned to pay attention and duck, but by this time I'd grown comfortable inside the shadowy space. The passageway made a couple of turns and branched off into directions I'd not yet explored before terminating in the boiler room, Brett's headquarters.

I expected to find Falcon kicked back with his feet propped on the desk, but when I turned the corner I saw him pacing about, waving his arms, talking loudly. "Too sweet to pass up, shit's bringing over two bucks a pound. We got this, bro."

Brett was nodding and listening, but turned when he saw me. Something in his eyes reminded me of an injured dog who wants help but will bite whoever tries. Stepping into the room brought an even greater surprise: Rosemary. Like Falcon, she appeared nervous, keyed up.

She said, "Oh, hey, Mr. Stiles. Wasn't expecting to see you here."

I hadn't seen her since the end of last school term and was shocked by her appearance. Her hair had been buzzed close on one side and left long on the other, with a purple streak extending to her shoulder. Metal studs protruded from beneath her lower lip. She was very thin and seemed much older, her eyes and mouth especially.

Falcon said, "Well I'll be damned. It's our old friend Lardass—I mean Bernie. What's up, dude?" Before I could answer he said, "Think fast," and let go another of his sidearm flings in my direction. He caught me off guard this time, and I was barely able to duck the flying object. It rang out against the wall behind me and landed next to a mop bucket.

I said, "What the fuck!" Then I turned to see what he'd thrown at my head. It lay there on the floor, a bright piece of metal larger than my thumb. I picked it up and saw that it was a petcock handle from one of the valves. It looked as if it had been polished with sandpaper.

"Feels good in your hand, don't it?" Falcon said. "Got some heft to it. That's brass in case you're wondering. Made in USA too. Hard to find pieces like that these days."

"Yeah, nice," I said. "Maybe you can make a medallion out of it and hang it around your neck." I tossed it back to him.

He dropped it into his pocket. "So tell me what's really goin' on, Bernie. I'm a little surprised to see you here. I figured you'd be all cozied up in your bedroom by now, in your momma's house. You do still live with your momma, don't you?"

"Actually no. My mother passed away three years ago."

"Oh. Sorry. But you're still in the same house, right?"

"That's right. I inherited it along with the mortgage, insurance payments, and maintenance responsibilities. All part of my cushy lifestyle."

His head bobbed a three-beat nod as he grabbed his crotch with his left hand and made a circular motion with his right. "I gotcha. Cool. But here you are in Brett's boiler room. I mean, that seems a little odd, if you don't mind me saying so. I hope you and my nephew ain't got some mutual masturbation thing going on."

"Ease off, Falcon," Rosemary said. "Mr. Stiles is cool, one of the best teachers I ever had." She smiled, reminiscing. "We used to get him off topic, and he always kept shit real. He could tell the best stories!" Her jaw and lips kept working after she'd spoken. She shifted her weight from side to side. "Still though, this does seem a little weird."

"Whatever you're thinking is wrong. Brett and I are friends. We talk, smoke, drink coffee. I could ask what you two are doing here. That seems weird to me."

Falcon cocked his head, raised an eyebrow, and turned to Rosemary, who was chewing something, possibly the inside of her cheek. "You're right, foxy girl. Bernie is cool, and sassy too. I like Bernie, always have. So I'll answer his question out of friendship." He pulled a cigarette from his shirt pocket and lit it, then turned to face me. His left hand kept going back to his crotch, and he shifted his hips as if he had an underwear problem. His cigarette hand resumed the circular pattern in time with his words. "It's like this, dude: we're here to help my young nephew work through some issues. You might say it's a family matter."

About that time I heard the squeak of the main door above us and footsteps on the ramp. I turned to see one of the crew entering the room, Travis Burrell. I'd taught him, a big surly boy, a few years back. He'd once threatened to beat my ass because I'd written him up for having simulated sex with a teddy bear he'd yanked out of a shy girl's book bag. He'd been humping the thing and moaning while I was trying to explain the grammatical concepts of coordination and subordination. I yelled at him, told him to get out. He tossed the stuffed toy back in the girl's face and sauntered across the room. "Sure, faggot," he said. "I don't need this shit anyway." Then he slammed the door.

In the principal's office he blew up in front of Mr. Palladar, called me a "lying fag," and said he'd beat the shit out of me. This got him placed in alternative school, and I didn't see him for a long time, until he was hired to work on the janitorial staff. I wasn't comfortable with his having access to my classroom, but I didn't think he was smart enough to devise a plan of sabotage. Still, I'd been purposely avoiding him.

Now he stood in front of me, holding a heavy tool bag. He stared for a second, then dropped the bag and turned to Falcon. "What's he doing here?"

"He was just leaving. Ain't that right, Bernie? Don't forget your coffee mug. Ain't that what you came after?"

Brett, looking pitiful, cleared his throat. "See ya later, Mr. Stiles."

"Okay, sure," I said, reaching to retrieve my mug from a cluttered shelf on the wall. "See you guys later. You too, Rosemary. Take care."

I left via the door at the top of the ramp, which opened onto a hallway lined with student lockers. It seemed less awkward than going back out through that pipe-laden service hall and less likely to arouse Travis's curiosity. I knew the locked entrance doors would open from the inside. My footsteps on the polished tile echoed off the thickly painted walls, adorned with posters and samples of student work. At the end of the empty corridor, I pressed against a smooth metal handle and stepped out into the cold, making sure the door shut behind me.

I'd been listening to a CD in the car, a metal band I knew Brett liked. When I turned the key it blared out a jarring crescendo before I could turn it off. I needed quiet. Dark forces were gathering in that boiler room. I wasn't born yesterday. Something was going down that could get Brett into a lot of trouble. Problem was, they knew that I knew.

I wanted Brett to believe I'd do anything for him. I wanted to show him that even when we feel powerless there are avenues of escape. A captured soldier's duty was to try to escape, but I'd never been a soldier. What could I do? I'd already tried to help him, and I'd sort of stood up to Falcon. That was something, and it would be easier to let it go at that. I looked down at my coffee-stained mug on the seat beside me. Inside was a polished brass handle like the one that bastard had thrown at me. I'd palmed it from the shelf when I retrieved the mug, and I was sure they hadn't seen. Thank God it was Friday and I didn't have to worry about planning lessons. I had other matters to think about.

The snug little house where I'd grown up was only a few blocks away. A lonely setting now—since Dad's fatal heart attack a decade ago and Mom's more recent final decline—it had been my refuge during troubled times and the place where I could drink coffee, smoke, and do my best thinking. But this was different.

Passing under a streetlight, the brass handle seemed to wink at me, a glint of yellow from inside the mug. A Thomas Paine quote flashed into my mind: "By perseverance and fortitude we have the prospect of a glorious issue; by cowardice and submission, the sad choice of a variety of evils. ..." I reached inside the mug, fingering the brass piece. It chinked against the side as I lifted it out. Falcon was right: its heft felt good. I squeezed the cool metal hard against my palm. At the next intersection I turned left to head back towards the police station in the middle of town rather than my house, knowing I'd be able to think along the way.

I held evidence in my hand of a petty heist in progress, hopefully enough to convince the police to go to the scene. They might even get a drug bust out of the deal. Explaining away Brett and Rosemary's involvement, along with what I was doing in that boiler room, were my main concerns. They were innocent victims of circumstance. Unwitting accomplices ... or unwilling? That's it! *Intimidated* would be my key word. And Falcon? Well, he was just petty—not to mention stupid—and about to go down, along with his surly sidekick. The prospect of this "glorious issue" made the possibility of an ass-kicking worth the risk. My brain hummed with the engine as I pressed the old sedan toward town. I switched the CD back on, letting the fortifying notes of Brett's metal music swell in my mind.

SYNCRETISM

UNCLE BART was my mother's only brother. Growing up, I'd seen him maybe once a year at family get-togethers, and I had noticed that he seemed to be aging faster than my other seldom-seen relatives, who remained sleek and fat between reunions. I had the opportunity during the last holiday season to spend some time with him while he was up from Florida visiting my mother, ostensibly on business although I never knew the specifics. I was getting ready for my final semester at the university and trying to think about the future. By that time Bart had become wizened and unkempt, full of irony, anger, and malicious humor, like Nick Nolte in his role as Father in *Hulk*.

My dad had died from a heart attack the year before and my sister had married and moved away to Birmingham, so Bart's presence in the house was not as inconvenient as it might have been. He was there for a week. I kept an apartment near campus, but during the break, I was in and out a lot, enjoying time spent relaxing in my childhood home and helping Mom get through the holidays.

Having this other male presence in the house was strange at first—sleeping in my sister's old room, shuffling through the kitchen in the mornings in pajamas and slippers, watching TV in the den with us, and taking his meals at the kitchen table. I soon realized that I hardly knew my Uncle Bart and was surprised to find a sense of humor and gentlemanly demeanor underneath his gruff sarcasm. After a few days, Mom and I both were enjoying having him around.

The three of us talked about politics, the economy, and the Middle East, but he didn't talk about himself much. Mom and I knew, although it was never stated, that he had no one to spend Christmas with. He had divorced four wives without producing any children, and the divorces weren't amicable. The most recent had occurred just this year, contributing significantly to his overall contemptuousness.

"Melba was a goal-oriented person," he commented one morning as we were finishing breakfast. "That's what attracted me to her initially. Problem was, her goal shifted from accruing personal wealth to my ruination. Damn near succeeded too." He took a drag off his Doral light, leaned in over his coffee mug, tapped his cigarette fingers to his gray temple. "I'm not as gullible as she thought, though. I had some holdings in Tampa and Panama City that she didn't know about. I landed on my feet, as I've managed to do over the years. But, enough of that. Tell me about your plans for the future, what you hope to do with an English degree."

Of course, I wanted to be a writer, like most everyone who majors in English. I hated telling people that, especially adult men who'd made lots of money. I didn't like their patronizing looks of mild amusement or their admonishments of, "Well, yes, but you'll need a back-up plan," so I usually said that I planned to teach or get into advertising or public relations. Bart's reaction, though, was not what I expected. In a sincere voice he added before I could answer, "Naturally, you'll want to write."

From the counter where she was rinsing plates and putting them in the dishwasher, Mom said, "Yes, but he needs a back-up plan. I've been telling him he should get his teaching certificate. He could get on at a high school close by and maybe even coach baseball. I don't know if you remember, Bart, but that boy used to love baseball."

He looked across the table at me and winked. Yes, he remembered, and I did too, the warm Thanksgiving afternoon we'd spent in my maw-maw's backyard playing catch while my great-uncles, aunts, and cousins sat around eating desserts and watching TV. He had sensed my boredom and initiated the conversation, which led to an intense session of glove-smacking burnout. "I hear you're a pretty good pitcher," he had said from a front porch rocker. "You'll have to show me what you got someday. I used to pitch myself, might could teach you a few of my old tricks."

I was twelve and shy, but my boredom and his seemingly genuine interest prompted an adventurous reply: "I've got a couple of gloves and a ball in the car."

He hopped up out of the rocker, and we ignored the grown-ups for the rest of the afternoon as he devoted his considerable energies to throwing and catching with me. Then it was time to go, and when I saw him again, I was a teenager and everything was different. Things were really different now. In the kitchen with Mom, Bart looked too decrepit to even play catch anymore. He took another drag on his cigarette then suffered a minor coughing spell. "I'm gonna quit these damn things one of these days," he said as the spasm subsided.

He got up and shuffled to the counter to pour more coffee. "Of course, Ann," he said to Mom, "he'll need a steady income, insurance, retirement, and so forth, but if he's got that writer thing in him, he'll need to get it out somehow. I think he should throw some energy into it now while he's young. Who knows, it just might lead to something. With talent, good material, and a little luck, a person can still make it writing and publishing." He sat back at the table and looked at me. "I'd like to see some of your work. I was an English major too, you know."

"I didn't know," I answered, trying not to show my surprise.

"Oh yes," he said, shaking another Doral from the pack. "I read all the classics, got especially interested in the American greats, from the Naturalists through the Modernists: Crane, London, Sinclair Lewis, Sherwood

Anderson, and of course Hemingway. He was my hero. I wanted to follow in his footsteps."

"So what did you do with yours? English degree, I mean."

"Oh, I never finished. I only needed a couple of quarters—we were on a quarter system back then—when I decided to take a break. Went down to Florida, got involved in some business ventures, and one thing led to another. Never made it back to school. Kept reading, though, and thinking about it—for a long time." His voice trailed off into despairing reflection.

I said, "Well, it's never too late. I've had classes with lots of people your age. They're called 'non-traditional' students—"

"Believe me, kid. It is too late for me. It's your turn now, to shine, to make your mark in the world. We'll talk about it more later, after I read some of your stuff."

My part-time employer, Java Chop, a coffee house and deli near campus, had called me in to work that day, so I decided to swing by the apartment when I got off to print out a copy of my latest story. The working title was "Eb and Flo, a Love Story about Nothing." It was an account of two androgynous characters who lead nondescript lonely lives, caring for their pets and following set routines until their chance meeting in a coffee shop. They each begin to organize their lives differently, to facilitate more "chance" meetings. They are slowly drawn into each other's world, and through their coffee-shop dialogue, the reader follows them on their journey to completeness. I was pretty proud of it and eager to show it to someone. Although I had doubts about Uncle Bart's critical skills and ability to appreciate what I was trying to accomplish, I hoped he would like it.

When I handed him the manuscript after supper, he appeared confused for a moment. As the recollection of our morning's conversation dawned, he said, "Oh, yes. Well now, this really looks like something. I can't wait to read it." He set the pages on the end table as he settled into an evening in front of the TV with Mom, watching their favorite investigative crime dramas. The next morning I noticed that the manuscript had been moved, but Bart made no mention of it during breakfast. It was the first weekday after the New Year holiday, and Mom had errands to run, gift returns mainly and an appointment for a pedicure. She seemed eager to get out of the house, plating up some Eggo waffles and microwaveable sausage patties instead of our usual bacon and eggs with grits and biscuits. As we ate and chatted about the weather and how bad the traffic was likely to be, I sensed Bart's eyes on me. I felt sure he had read the story and was examining me for structural flaws, signs of weakness that he was preparing to reveal.

I began to dread the moment of Mom's leaving, of being left alone with him, and I tried to think of an excuse to leave with her. As she was putting on her coat and checking her purse to be sure she had the receipts, Bart looked at me. "So, it seems we have some time on our hands, alone, like old bachelors. An opportunity to ... discuss things." He raised an eyebrow diabolically, like an evil professor, then grinned. "I enjoyed the story. I'm impressed with your talent."

Mom said, going out the door, "Bye fellows. You two try to behave while I'm gone. I'll be back late this afternoon."

When I answered, "Bye, Mom," a small spasm of apprehension passed out of my body. He had said he liked the story, that I had talent. I was surprised at how much this mattered, and I worked—at that moment and at times throughout the morning—to not let my need for his approval show.

He pressed the door closed behind Mom. "C'mon, let me pour you another cup of coffee before we get started." As he shuffled across the floor in his slippers and baggy pajamas, I noticed his grizzled whiskers, his gossamer hair charged with static and standing off his head, but I also saw a light in his blue eyes I hadn't seen before, a disconcerting impishness. "Let's sit in the den," he said, "where we'll be comfortable."

He disappeared for a second as I tried to relax in my usual chair. When he returned, he was holding the "Eb and Flo" manuscript. He tossed it onto the coffee table and sat across from me on the sofa. "You've got some pretty good chops. On a sentence by sentence level this is right up there. It's musical, lyrical, metaphorical, and all that. Your transitions transition and you're able to do what all writers struggle with: move people in and out of rooms. But ... the story is still lacking. In spite of your good writing, it's a flop."

I exhaled heated air from my burst bubble. "Well, thanks, I guess. For being honest—"

"But don't despair. I've got what you and all writers need: *material*. I'm giving you a gift today, the gift of narrative thrust. Conflict, action, suspense, tension, drama—that's what it's all about." He eased back into the cushions, reached for his cigarettes and lighter. "You might want to take notes."

∽

BACK IN THE SEVENTIES Uncle Bart had been a student at the same college I attended. Aaron-Maslow had a wild reputation then, the number one party school in the state. He had begun as a serious student, a lover of literature with writing skills he hoped to develop. He attended on a full-ride scholarship—baseball and academics. He was full of promise and optimism in spite of the toxic political climate of that era and the increasing scope of domestic and international disasters. But after three years of college life—the stress of playing ball, staying in shape, and keeping up his grades in a cornucopia of sex, drugs, and rock and roll—he found himself on academic probation, no longer on the baseball team, and broke.

He was tall and good-looking with thick blonde hair to his collar and a mustache. He had managed to stay away from the heavy drinking, pot, and other drugs throughout his freshman year, but with lots of pretty girls and a party somewhere every night, the temptation became too much for a young man who had previously led a sheltered life. His hair grew, his manner of dress changed, and he formed new friendships with people who weren't so hung up about grades and sports.

Bart had seen Davis around campus and had even had classes with him but didn't get to know him until one night in May when he found himself at a party where the lithe and swarthy hippie was the center of attention. Upwards of 100 people—an assortment of freaks including students, faculty, and dropouts—had gathered at an old farmhouse a few miles outside of town. People were drinking and laughing on the porch, in the yard, and in clusters throughout the rambling structure. The main hive of activity, though, seemed to be back in the kitchen. Groups kept moving in and out of there in huddled discussion over loud strains of Led Zeppelin. Bart guessed the reason for the activity, and his theory was confirmed after he edged his way into the room to get another beer out of an ice-filled tub. Davis was leaning over the high Formica-covered counter, his straight black hair pulled back in a ponytail. He was flanked by a seriously interested group that seemed a bit younger than the rest, probably freshmen, two girls and a chubby guy with pink cheeks. Davis was holding forth, laughing, cutting his eyes from one to another, and showing them something on the counter. He was providing reassurance; then Bart saw them make the exchange: money passed into Davis's hands, then swiftly into his jeans. The chubby guy said, "Thanks, man." Davis responded by wrapping his arms around all three. "You guys are beautiful," he said. "Enjoy, and let me know when you need more."

Bart, hanging around the beer tub, became interested in watching this guy work. They exchanged glances once or twice as Davis displayed his charm through a steady stream of customers in groups and pairs, some excited and some apprehensive. There were lots of girls at the party and most of them at some point made their way to either Davis and his place at the counter or the beer tub. Bart, maintaining his vantage point, soon found himself in conversation with a hippie girl, breathtaking in her beauty.

She had reached into the tub, pulled up a dripping longneck, then tossed her head to settle her shag haircut back into place. In response to Bart's stare, she smiled, flashing her big hazel eyes at his. "Hi. You keeping watch over the beer?"

"Oh. Yeah, I guess. This is an interesting place to stand. All the cool people end up in this room at some point. Here. Let me open that for you."

He reached toward her bottle with an opener. She met him halfway and held the bottle firmly while he popped the top. Moving closer brought a slight misalignment in his mind. Her appearance suggested an herbal, organic smell, but her fragrance was more like expensive *Parisienne parfum*.

"Thanks," she said with another slight head toss. He noticed the silver hoop earrings shaking against her fair skin. Thickly layered strands of hair the color of polished white ash swooped over her ears then followed her slender neck down between her shoulders. She smiled and let her eyes linger on his face for a moment. "So, when you say 'cool people' are you including that long-haired dude over there at the counter?"

"Sure, why not? I mean, he's been the most popular guy at the party ever since I've been here."

"Hmm … that's interesting. Any idea what his secret is?"

"Not sure, but I'd guess he has something other people want."

"Hmmph!" She knitted her brows in mock seriousness. "You don't suppose he's selling drugs over there do you?"

"Well, since his jeans pockets are stuffed with cash, that seems a definite possibility."

She sidled a step closer and lowered her voice to a whisper. "What do you think he's selling?"

"No idea. Something twisted up in tiny little plastic bags."

Someone in the other room put on a new album and they became aware of the beginnings of a much gentler tune that featured acoustic guitar, lilting vocals, and textured instrumentation. "Far-out!" she said, "Tull." She sucked in her lower lip, half-closed her eyes, and moved her head to the flowing rhythm. "Ian Anderson's a genius," opening her eyes to his. "What do you think?"

"Great, I love Tull!" As soon as he had spoken, he felt that he had let too much excitement show over their having such a small thing in common.

She nodded and smiled, glanced back to Davis, who was relaxing between customers at the counter. "I think I'll mosey over and see what this guy's up to." She turned and he watched her walk away in her cut-off jeans and clog sandals.

A couple of guys he knew came into the kitchen with bags of ice and another case of beer to replenish the tub. Bart exchanged pleasantries and helped with the task. When he stood up and looked over at Davis and the girl, he saw that she was leaning into him, his arm around the small of her back, lifting her short denim jacket and exposing a pair of dimples just above the top of her hip-hugger shorts. With a hand against his chest she pushed herself away and turned, smiling, to look at Bart. With one arm around Davis's waist, she motioned with the other for Bart to come over. Making the few steps across the room, Bart noticed that Davis was also smiling at him, as if they were complicit in some scheme that was just beginning to hatch.

The girl said, "You were right. This character has been up to no good. I interrogated him and he confessed."

"Guilty as charged, your honor," Davis said. "Question is, what are you gonna do to me."

She grinned. "Help you spend the money, of course." She nodded toward Bart. "He had you pegged all along. He's an undercover investigator, you know."

"Undercover … that explains it, why I've seen him hanging around the student center in the afternoons, and carrying books in and out of the library." He smiled warmly, looked at Bart with eyes the color of dark chocolate. "Now that you've nailed me, I guess you should know my name." He reached out his hand. "I'm Davis."

Bart took the hand in the accepted thumb-locking hippie grasp. "Bart. Pleased to meet you."

He looked at the girl. "I don't know your name."

She tilted her head causing one hoop earring to dangle, the other to lie against her neck. "Mary. Simple and easy to remember."

They drank and chatted in the crowded kitchen, mainly about the assorted characters who continued to come and go. Mary was animated, doing most of the talking. Several times when partygoers approached Davis with furtive glances and veiled questions, he shrugged his shoulders, smiled, and held up empty hands. Mary asked, "Are you all sold out?"

"Almost," he answered, with an implication in his eyes.

She said, "Uh-huh," then turned to Bart. "So, what did you say you were majoring in?"

"I didn't. Haven't had a chance yet."

"Let me guess. I'd say you're of a practical turn of mind. And you have a sadness in your eyes for all that's been lost. And your body—" she eyed him up and down—"suggests physical robustness. I think you're someone who climbs around on mountainsides and in valleys digging up rocks, looking for fossils. You, my new friend Bart, are a geology major."

Bart chuckled. "That's a very interesting guess. Your insightfulness is staggering. But, unfortunately, you're not even close."

"She does that all the time," Davis said. "She guessed somebody right last year at a party and hasn't been able to stop since. She is a great judge of human nature. Now, if she could only match the natures up with the right humans … ."

She laughed and pressed against Davis. "I figured you out pretty quick, though, didn't I? I guess that's what really matters."

"Well, you're right about me being what matters most, but I'm not as transparent as you think. There are some nooks and crannies in my psyche that you haven't peered into yet."

"There he goes, talking about his psyche. Davis is a psychology major, as you might have guessed."

Bart said, "I would have never known. I'd have placed him in the business department. He seems to have mastered the laws of supply and demand."

As they laughed, drank, and smoked their cigarettes, Bart noticed the mood of the party changing. Movement and noise subsided, replaced by a subdued camaraderie. Pink Floyd oozed from the speakers. Mellow. Joints were circulating everywhere in the smoky house, and people seemed content in their various groupings, engaged in deep conversation. "Our work here is done," Davis said. "Why don't we split, get out under the stars, and enjoy the great outdoors." He looked at Bart. "Come on, Man. I've got some things to show you."

It was indeed a beautiful night, even when viewed from the inside of Davis's old pickup. The three of them rode together through scenic rural areas Bart had never seen before. The truck, a Dodge from the 1950s, was battered and noisy but seemed eager for the changing terrain, the washed-out curvy blacktops and steep hills. They turned onto a dirt road that after a few miles became barely passable. Picking their way over harsh bumps and ruts, they approached a wooden bridge that spanned an energetic rocky creek. Davis eased the truck over the planks, water gurgling beneath them, then pulled over and killed the engine and lights. The trees on either side were black and looming under the full moon. The road was mottled black with shadows, lumpy with rocks and potholes.

They had just finished smoking a very potent joint, and Bart was suddenly struck with a wave of paranoia. What the hell were they doing? Who were these people? Were they going to kill him and leave his body out here? Perform some weird ritual? These thoughts flurried through his guts, producing body tremors he could scarcely conceal. They sat quietly in the truck for a few moments before Davis began rummaging around under the seat. Finally he said, "Here it is," bringing up something in his hand.

Mary said, "Cool. I'm glad you brought that. Lemme have it." She snatched the roll of toilet paper from him and nudged Bart with her knee and elbow. "Open the door, dude. I gotta pee."

He exhaled, almost laughed, and pressed down on the Vise-Grip pliers that served as a door handle. Davis opened his door and got out also. Mary stepped gingerly over the ditch and disappeared into some bushes. Davis came around to Bart's side and handed him a beer. The air was filled with the sound of running water, crickets, frogs, owls, and other night creatures. They each lit a cigarette and listened for a moment. Davis said, "Snake creek. Cool, huh?"

"Far-out … literally."

Davis slapped Bart on the shoulder. "I'm glad you like my back yard."

From Davis's smile Bart couldn't tell if he was serious or not; then he heard Mary approaching. She handed Davis the toilet paper.

He said, "Why don't you roll us another joint while I fix up a little something else for us."

Mary said, "Sure," and got back inside the truck.

Davis turned his back to Bart and, bending over the Dodge fender, began to make preparations. When Bart stepped in closer, he could see three individual sheets of toilet paper placed side by side. Davis removed his large black wallet, attached to his belt with a chain, and dug deep into one of the compartments. "When I saw how sales were going back there, I decided to stash a little for personal use, enough to divide up three ways, a good number—Biblical, you know." He placed the small twist-tied package, made from the cut-off corner of a sandwich bag, on the fender. It was mashed flat from being in his wallet.

"What is that, anyway," Bart asked. "I don't mess with hard drugs."

Davis grinned in the moonlight, his teeth flashing white. "It's not heroin, if that's what you're thinking. It's the love drug, MDA, kind of a combination of acid and speed. It's great, really mellow. Makes everything all better."

"But I'm short of funds tonight—"

"Don't worry about it. This one's on me. It's not that expensive anyway."

"But we don't really know each other … why did you pick me—"

Again the flash of white. "I trust Mary's instincts. She's a great judge of human nature, remember?"

Davis's hands were busy. "Here," he said. "Hold this lighter up so I can see." He used the blade of his pocketknife to measure equal portions of the white powder into the center of each toilet paper sheet. He wet his fingers and made three little balls, wrapping the tissue around the drug. The passenger door hinges creaked as Mary climbed out with a freshly rolled joint.

Davis said, "Cool, baby. Go ahead and light that thing up. We're gonna find God tonight." He handed Bart and Mary each a little drug ball and kept one for himself. Holding it up just prior to popping it into his mouth, he said, "Shall we?"

Bart glanced at Mary. She winked, swallowed down her drug with a big gulp of beer. He did the same.

〜

HE HAD NEVER SEEN anything as beautiful as fire, Bart thought later, except for Mary's face as she laughed and talked inside Davis's teepee. His was one of five spread out along the grassy banks beside the creek, a little community not far from the bridge where he had stopped the truck. As they had topped the last rise in the old Dodge, bringing the teepees into view, Bart had expressed his surprise: "What the—"

"My front yard," Davis had said.

"You mean you live here?"

"Yep. Great views, cool neighbors, and really cheap rent."

Davis and Mary explained, as they parked the Dodge at the edge of the meadow, that Dr. Ostrakan of the psychology department owned the land and had agreed to the teepee settlement as kind of an experiment, a "simple living" collective. The professor didn't care what they did as long as they didn't erect permanent structures and took care of their garbage.

"It's amazing," Bart said. "That you can live this way. I'd have never thought—"

"It does have its downside. It was great last summer when we built everything, but over the winter things got kinda rough. Some nights we stayed in town at Mary's place."

Bart registered surprise. Mary answered, "Yeah, my parents don't know about any of this. They still pay for my apartment and expenses, thinking I'm the model college girl. If they knew I flunked out this term, they'd shit bricks. I won't be able to keep it a secret forever, though."

"Let's don't worry about that stuff," Davis said. "Tonight ...," he made an expansive gesture, "the sky, the creek, us. This is what matters now."

As the drug dissolved and found its way into his bloodstream and brain, Bart felt a dawning realization that Davis was right, that this—the here and now—was what mattered most. With childlike excitement he helped Davis build the fire, bringing in sticks of wood from the stack outside. Then he watched Davis's expert hands as he prepared the kindling and laid the sticks just so in the rock-lined pit.

As the fire crackled and popped, the smoke, heavy and slow at first, began to find its way out the top. Mary's face with the firelight reflected in her eyes, the music of her voice, and Davis's reassuring smile had combined to produce a feeling of contentment unlike anything Bart had ever known. Now, with the fire burning clean, flames dancing over a bed of glowing embers, the contentment was still there, radiating out to blend with the heat of the fire and the warm souls of his new friends he had met only a few hours before. Amazing. Love, that's what it was. Bart was experiencing true love—he was sure—for the first time in his life.

The fire melted all reserve between them and for a long time they shared stories from their lives, their childhoods, hopes, and fears. Mary was the first member of her family to attend college. She had a little brother with Down Syndrome and other developmental problems. Mary had stuttered and been shy as a child but had miraculously blossomed through the loving encouragement of her fifth-grade teacher. Davis was a surviving identical twin. The brother had died in a car wreck when they were toddlers, cracking his head on the metal dashboard. Davis, standing next to his mother in the front seat, had been saved by her partially restraining arm, extended before impact, an arm that had not been strong enough to hold both boys back from death. Davis had been cut and broken. He pulled up his tee shirt to show a star-shaped pattern of white scars on his chest and ribcage.

Bart felt that he didn't have much to share from his sheltered life. He had stayed clean, made good grades, played ball, went to church a lot. He'd never suffered anything, really, other than the scrapes and bruises of a childhood that seemed too normal. But he wanted to share; he wanted to give them something of himself, so he told about his dream of becoming a writer, how he felt that he was born to do something important, to leave part of himself behind after he was gone. He sometimes imagined books he had authored on library shelves waiting to be discovered by new readers generations from now, and he sometimes dreamed books, but so far he had not been able to capture them upon waking, only bits and pieces he had used to construct stories. He had written several stories he was proud of. He told Mary and Davis they could read them some time, that he would be honored.

They listened. Mary leaned forward, smiling, big eyes looking over the impish flames at Bart. "So now I've got it. Your physical robustness is for living and experiencing all life has to offer, to get it into books; the sadness in your eyes is for the human condition and your need to make sense of it. You, my friend, must be an English major!"

They laughed. Davis said, "My God, Mary, you're clairvoyant! Our very souls laid bare beneath your gaze!"

As the chuckles subsided Mary said, "That's really cool. English is my minor, majoring in art. Did I say that yet? Was, I mean. Was majoring in art before I flunked out. Anyway, I love to read, and I write poems sometimes. I'm surprised I never saw you in the humanities building."

"Probably because my classes are always early in the morning. We have to get our classes over so we can spend the afternoons practicing."

"Practicing?"

"Yeah, I'm on the baseball team. Was, I mean."

"Wow, a real jock! But I guess that must be tough. All the responsibility, people counting on you."

Bart didn't know what to say.

Davis said, "So, dude, that is cool. I read a lot myself. Who are your favorite authors?"

That got the words flowing again. Bart told about Hemingway and his quest for one true sentence, about Flannery O'Conner and her Jesus-twisted characters, Tom Robbins and his far-flung metaphors. Each time he mentioned a book or author, Davis and Mary nodded their enthusiastic agreement and exclaimed, "Cool!" or "Far-out!" They were readers too, loved Vonnegut and Brautigan as much as he did. The discovery of their common interests was a wave that carried comfort like soft caramel throughout his body, and the night passed, slowly and wonderfully, inside the teepee.

The floor, constructed from planks salvaged from warehouse pallets, was strewn with old quilts, sleeping bags, and pillows; there was a chair, a mirror, and several shelves, one of which held a softly glowing kerosene lamp, another a wash basin. Plenty of fresh, gurgling water running just outside; warmth inside. Cold beer in the cooler, fine Columbian weed in Mary's batik bag—what else could anyone need?

The sky, visible through the smoke hole, slowly changed from deep purple to gray, and the stars faded. The sedative effect of the beer was beginning to hold sway over the diminishing effects of the MDA, and, after eating roasted wieners and a big pan of popcorn popped on the fire, the three were nearly talked out. Davis turned out the lamp then began to snuggle with Mary in what seemed to be their usual sleeping area. Bart reclined a couple of feet away, resting his head on a rolled-up blanket.

The fire had burned down to mostly coals now, three charred sticks producing a flickering medley of blue and orange. Bart closed his eyes, but inside his skull there was still much activity. The drug and the night's revelations allowed only a measure of relaxation; sleep remained outside, a foreigner patiently awaiting entry. He listened to the soft popping and hissing of the dying fire, and from Davis and Mary's blankets he heard murmurs and whispers that blended with the gurgling of the creek just beyond the canvas wall. From out there he heard frogs croaking as the night slipped away, along with owls, whippoorwills, barking foxes, and an occasional splash in the creek, but these animal sounds were slowly displaced by the sounds of Davis and Mary cooing and caressing under their blankets.

The murmurs became moans of pleasure, then pants and grunts as the couple made love beside him. He was outside their zone of passion, yet he felt a part of it. His pulse was synchronized with their rhythm, and he imagined the sensations of their mounting pleasure. He did not feel shame, embarrassment, or the need to turn away, but rather contentment, lying there with his eyes closed, wrapped in the warmth of the fire, blankets, and love.

As the tempo beside him increased, so did the volume and pitch of Mary's panting. Their movement became strained, a struggle for release, and Mary yelped with pleasure. Bart felt something stir beside him, then pressure against his arm. Mary's fingers were pressing, making circles on his wrist. Then her hand found his and squeezed tightly as she stepped over the edge into a free-fall of pleasure. As the grunting and panting subsided, the sounds outside became audible again. Bart drifted off to sleep, holding Mary's warm, relaxed hand.

Before a week had passed the three of them were on their way to Florida. Davis suggested the move in a way that seemed natural, considering their current academic standing and future prospects. They loaded their most necessary and cherished possessions—amp, turntable, speakers, albums, Native American artifacts, a few pieces of handmade pottery, baseball gloves, camping gear, jeans, tees, and several boxes of Mary's clothes—under a makeshift camper on the back of the old Dodge and headed south to Panama City. The general idea was to be bums, to sleep on the beach until they could find jobs and a cheap place. They'd be getting there between spring break and the summer vacation rush, the ideal time to seek out opportunities. Davis was persuasive, Mary seemed excited, and Bart was unable to resist.

〰

TIME PASSED AND MY UNCLE BART ended up staying in Florida, until the last month of his life, living out his days with sea gulls, the sound of the surf, and beach music in the background. He spent the years getting married and divorced and pursuing a variety of business ventures including nightclubs, car lots, and liquor stores from the western end of the panhandle down to Tampa. He did drugs, drank, and smoked until a few weeks after he critiqued my story in Mom's den, when he was diagnosed with lung cancer, already in the advanced stages. This would be the first spring break in many years that he would not spend on the Gulf.

After an obligatory round of chemo did nothing but make his hair fall out and leave him sicker, Mom contacted the hospice agency. A bed was set up—in my old room this time as it allowed easier access—and Bart was moved in as the dogwoods reached full bloom. He didn't put up much of a struggle, letting the nurses, Mom, and the morphine have their way. During those last days he seemed to enjoy, more than anything, my company. At first I sought reasons to stay away from the house, a place that was taking on the smell of death in spite of Mom's opening the windows to the spring breezes. I tried to immerse myself in work during my last schedule of classes before graduation, but after a week or so of trying to avoid the inevitable, I gave in and cleared my calendar of obligations for several afternoons.

Mom left us alone as much as possible, and we talked about literature and writing, the mysteries of life, and the amorphous webbing that binds us together with everything else in the universe. He laughed and was in good cheer most of the time, but he occasionally drifted off into staring, silent reflection. He was sharing deeply from the well of his collected musings, but he seemed to be struggling to go deeper.

When we had gone down to his beach-front bungalow at the end of the Perdido Key strip, just east of Gulf Shores, to bring him back to Georgia, we left most of his possessions for later and shut up the little house. But he had insisted on bringing a few personal items. There was a thick cardboard storage box, the kind made for holding files and records. It was battered and taped at the corners and the lid was sealed with layers of clear tape. As Mom was packing his slippers, toiletries, and necessary items, he elbowed me and pointed to the box sitting on the floor at the foot of his unmade bed. "That's coming too. Me and that box have got to leave here together. Go ahead and put it in the trunk."

I lifted the heavy box as he asked, without thinking much about its contents, and it rode with us back to Georgia. Bart's final weeks slipped by, and I didn't think of the box again until the afternoon when he told me to drag it out of the closet and open it up. I pulled out my knife and started to cut through the tape.

Breathing deeply from the oxygen tube at his nostrils, he said, "Everything you'll need is in there." I lifted the lid and he added, "The stuff of life."

The box was filled with notebooks.

"I took notes, kept journals," Bart said weakly from his bed. "I always planned to sift through it, sort it out into stories and maybe a novel, but … I ran out of time. That's all that's left of me now. Not much to show for a life, is it?"

I groped for words. "You were a businessman. You provided goods and services. You helped other people to be happy and live their lives. That counts."

"Goods and services. I guess that's what it boils down to after all."

I ran my hand along the spiral backs and cardboard covers, pulling one out into the light. The notebook was labeled in black magic marker on the cover. Neat block letters spelled out the word, "Environment." The next one in the stack was labeled, "Lust." I pulled out several more notebooks, each cover printed with a one-word title. Before I stopped and put the lid back on I saw these words: *Crime, Jealousy, Punishment, Resistance, Revenge, Deceit, Murder* …. There were lots of notebooks in there, but that was enough for now. "Wow," I said, "interesting titles."

Bart's eyelids sagged over irises that had grown dull. "Yes. At least I had that. An interesting life. I was never bored, until now. This dying business is starting to get old." He drifted off into a deep sleep from which he never fully awoke. A few days later he was gone.

After the sparsely attended funeral I carried the box to my apartment and parked it within reach of my futon. When I pulled off the lid, my hand went straight to the last title I had seen: *Murder*. I had to know if Uncle Bart had been a bad man. I suspected that he had, but, oddly—and I struggled with admitting this to myself—I didn't love him any less for it. The notebook paper was yellowing around the edges, each page filled with Bart's sloppy yet legible cursive. I read the first page carefully, skimmed ahead, then went back and read slowly. The notebook was indeed a first-person account of a murder that had been committed in the winter of 1976.

The victim was a sick old reprobate, proprietor of Ray Ballard's Beachside Motel. He had provided Davis, Mary, and Bart a place to stay in exchange for their help in operating the establishment. The old man had other business interests and a trophy wife in her forties whose needs were not being met and with whom Bart found favor. Davis managed to charm his way into the old man's confidence: Ballard, after an evening of drunken camaraderie with Davis, showed him a special stash in the maintenance shed that nobody, not even the wife, knew about. The scheme, according to the narrative, was Davis's idea, but its enactment required Bart's participation. He kept the wife occupied while Davis got the old man drunk then smothered him in his sleep. The wife was satisfied, upon discovering her husband dead the next morning, that he had died from natural causes. He had been in poor health for some time, and now she could collect the insurance. A few days after the funeral, the young trio left the widow to her fortune, and made off with considerable loot, including boxes of war relics: Confederate belt buckles, bullets, canteens; gas masks from WWI; German Iron Cross and Swastika medals;

a Samurai sword; Japanese Nambu and German Luger pistols; and various helmets, patches, uniforms, emblems, and flags. They also got away with a gallon jar filled with silver dollars. No investigation was ever launched.

What Davis, Mary, and Bart did afterward is another story, or maybe several. I'll have to spend some time sorting it out. I'll have the opportunity to do that now since Bart's will named Mom and me as his only beneficiaries. He left her enough to allow for a comfortable early retirement, and she plans to move to Birmingham to be near my sister and the grandbaby that will be here in time for the holidays. Bart left me the beach house and $100,000. I look forward to moving down there after graduation and getting some writing done.

SHADOW OF DEATH

"LISTEN, RACHEL," Celeste said, setting her wine glass gently on the tabletop, "I don't usually talk about my cases—you know that—but this one is keeping me up nights. I feel like I'll explode if I don't vent to someone."

"I'm all ears, but what about confidentiality?"

"It's okay. I won't use their real names. I don't think you'll recognize the story. It wasn't in the news that much, and it's been a while." She broke eye contact, then contemplated her hands as they encircled the base of her glass, searching for her former confidence. She'd achieved so much, but her dream of establishing a successful practice in family and child psychology had become a nightmare.

The friends were having dinner at Angelo's, a downtown pizzeria and bar where they had been meeting since their college days. "This girl," Celeste said, "continues to regress in spite of my best efforts, in spite of medication even. But now I think I finally know why. Problem is, I'm powerless. I don't know what to do next."

"That doesn't sound like you," Rachel said, gesturing for the waiter. "You've always known what to do, about everything."

Celeste smiled. "This is different. I've never had a case that presented so many dilemmas—professional, ethical, legal, moral, even spiritual for Christ's sake."

Rachel slid her glass in front of her as she leaned forward. "Fascinating." When she blinked, one eye lid lagged behind the other, resembling a lazy wink.

"There were problems in the family before the father's death, and the daughter—I'll call her Annie—was having trouble in school as early as second grade, when her brother was born. Up to that point she'd been the only child, the center of attention, daddy's little girl."

Rachel signaled the waiter again with an impatient finger. The heavy young man stopped at their booth. "Would you like more salad? Breadsticks?" His long black hair covered half his face. He carried menus in one hand and an empty tray in the other.

"Yes." Rachel said. "And another glass of Merlot, please."

"Merlot also, for me." Celeste turned back to her friend. "Things went downhill after the other child was born."

"No problem," the waiter said. "And will there be anything else?"

"Just bring a carafe," Rachel said. "I've got a feeling we're going to be here awhile."

"Fairly typical, really," Celeste said, breaking off a piece of bread from a small loaf, "for a child to become passive-aggressive, hostile even, after the birth of a sibling, but *Annie's* behavior went beyond normal. Her mother started getting calls from school. Annie this, Annie that—not doing her work, damaging property, fighting. The child never did adjust. That's how I first got involved with the case. School system called me in to interpret some test results."

"Sounds like she'd been spoiled, maybe, before the other kid came along. My niece was the same way—"

"Not really. They were a working-class family. Dad was a construction superintendent, worked all the time. Mom stayed home. They carried on for a long time, working, taking care of the kids, paying the bills, meeting with teachers, until Annie reached middle school. That's when the marriage started falling apart."

Rachel smoothed a strand of dark hair behind her ear. "What happened? Dad start cheating?"

"No, worse. He became abusive." Celeste stopped, checking an impulse to reach into her purse for a cigarette. There was no smoking in the restaurant, and she had quit a year ago. There were still times, though, when the old habit tried to reestablish itself. She took another bite of bread and drained her wine glass. "He was the dominant male type. Liked to hunt and fish, drove a big four-wheel drive. Couldn't engage his wife in meaningful dialogue about the family dynamics, about her needs. He didn't see the signs, or failed to acknowledge them. Like many men who fit that profile, he tried to force the circumstances, make them fit his paradigm." Celeste stopped when she realized she'd touched a nerve. Rachel had recently divorced a man much like the one she was describing. Her friend was slowly turning her wine glass on the tabletop, looking into it.

"Sounds familiar," Rachel said.

"Yeah … well, anyway, the wife had been so busy taking care of the family and dealing with Annie's problems that her own needs weren't being met. She started working part-time as a receptionist for an orthodontist, and he began to show an interest."

"Good for her."

"Yes, it was good for her, until her husband found out."

"Uh-oh, not good. How bad?"

Their corner booth was dimly lit by a candle that flickered on a wrought iron sconce, casting the brick wall it was mounted on into textured relief. "It was pretty bad." Celeste looked at the shadows, remembering the home visit when she had seen the mother's face: split lip, black eyes still puffy and swollen.

"Well?" Rachel said, calling Celeste back. "What happened after? I mean, after he beat the shit out of her. Did she leave him or kill him? That's it, isn't it? She killed the abusive bastard!"

"No, no, no. Nothing like that, and as far as I know, the abuse only happened once. But that one time was serious enough—neighbors took her to the emergency room— for the courts to get involved. That's how I got called in. They had decided to try and save the marriage, to keep the family intact, and they obviously needed help."

The waiter arrived and placed salad, bread, and wine on the tabletop. He smiled, looking above them at the brick wall. "Will there be anything else?"

"No," Celeste said. "We're good now, thanks."

Rachel reached for the carafe. "Why would she want to salvage an abusive relationship if there was someone else? She had the orthodontist, right?"

"He dumped her. Decided to protect his face, I guess, after he saw what happened to hers."

"Typical male. Get out when it stops being convenient."

"Right, typical. It's all really very typical, isn't it?"

"Seems that way to me. Must be like … well, dozens of other cases you've handled. I don't see why you're so worked up over this one."

"It's about the daughter, remember?"

"Right. Regressing. So how did she handle her mother getting beaten?"

Celeste's eyes moved from her friend's face to the tabletop. Her hands holding the wine glass made a wavering shadow over the salad bowl. She began to sift through memories of the girl—Allison was her real name—and how she had changed over the last two years from a sullen, underachieving preteen to a deeply disturbed adolescent. She saw the angry red welts and scars up and down the insides of Allison's forearms where she had scraped and cut herself. Rachel wanted to hear the story, to be entertained. Celeste wanted to be free of it. There were parts she couldn't tell, that couldn't be communicated no matter how much wine they drank. How would she be able to convey the chill she had felt when Allison told her, finally, about what happened that night? How could she describe those dead eyes looking out from black shadow, a manifestation of the shame that was metastasizing inside of her?

It had been clear from the beginning that Allison hated her father, what he had become and how he had hurt her mother. The man seemed clueless, and he never did take responsibility for what he had done. In the ways of appeasement and emotional expression he was a blunderer, finally turning to alcohol and drugs to escape the frustration of a reality he could not control—a response that could only make things worse.

Celeste remembered that first home visit when she had gone up to Allison's room to get a sense of the child, her emotional state. She had left the parents sitting at opposite ends of a distressed brown sofa while the little boy played on the floor with a plastic truck. She followed the daughter up the staircase to her room. Celeste knew that the preteen and early adolescent years were a time when children became adept at posturing and posing for adults to conceal the turmoil inside, the dark secrets, the desires they often felt should be hidden from those who had nurtured them through the earlier innocent years. Celeste hoped that the intimate physical space would reveal parts of Allison's personality she had otherwise learned to hide.

The room seemed typical: decorated in pink and purple with bean bags, flowery inflatable cushions, and throw pillows everywhere. Frilly bed with a psychedelic flower-print comforter. Shoes, jeans and tee shirts spilling out of the closet. Posters on the wall: Miley Cyrus, One Direction, The Beatles. And there were holdovers from earlier periods. A play kitchen made of pink plastic was crammed into a corner and stacked with magazines, school books, CD cases, and handbags. Stuffed animals—kittens, puppies, and a sad-eyed panda—gazed expectantly from the clutter. A furry lemur with Velcro hands hung from the closet door knob.

"This is it," Allison said. Then, motioning to the bed, "You can sit down if you want to." She plopped down in a bean bag, picked up a remote from the floor, and clicked on a portable TV atop her chest of drawers. It came on loudly, a Disney sitcom with canned laughter.

"I think we could talk better with that off," Celeste said.

"Why? Don't you know how to multitask? I thought psychologists were smart."

Celeste could only remember bits of the conversation. It had not been productive, nor had their subsequent visits. Looking over the salad bowl and breadsticks at Rachel's face, she realized that her entire involvement with the case—two years of work—had been a waste of time: the father was dead; the mother was bungling her parenthood role, relying on sleep aids, antidepressants, and pain medication to get through each day; the little boy was subject to tantrums, bullying his first-grade classmates; and the daughter was clinically depressed, even suicidal. If she had it all to do over, she would handle things differently. There had been signs, she realized, that pointed to a different course.

She remembered in Allison's room the framed picture lying face down on the nightstand. There had been other pictures, snapshots of Allison with friends and with her mother, on the walls and on a little white shelf. A framed photo on her chest of drawers showed Allison smiling with her arms around a large golden retriever. Her face was pressed next to the dog's, her hand under the muzzle, holding the head up for the camera. The dog seemed old and tired.

Celeste had not seen any animals, either outside or in the house. "Looks like a nice dog," she said. "Do you still have it?"

"No. Sally's gone." Her eyes narrowed. When she spoke, she barely opened her mouth. "Daddy did something with her, just 'cause she got old. I don't know what. I know what he did to the puppies, though."

"Puppies?" Celeste asked from the edge of Allison's bed. "When did you have puppies?"

"It wasn't that long ago. Daddy killed them."

Celeste was barely able to mask her heightened interest. "Why did he do that? He must have had a reason."

The girl stared at the TV screen as she talked. "He said they'd be better off, that they were gonna die anyway. I could have saved them, though."

Allison was reluctant to talk about it, but Celeste, through careful questioning, pulled out the story of three sickly puppies—one with a lump on its side—born to an old, uninterested dog. Allison had watched as her dad duct-taped a vacuum cleaner hose to the exhaust of his truck and placed the other end, along with the puppies, under an overturned cardboard box. He had told her that he was putting them to sleep, that they wouldn't feel a thing.

There was no evidence of the father in Allison's room. No family pictures of the four of them together, although there were some shots of the little brother. On the far side of the chest of drawers almost out of sight was a trashcan stuffed with broken Happy Meal toys, various body parts of dolls, and ripped-apart picture books. Kids Allison's age, in striving for maturity, often wanted to distance themselves from childish things. Celeste had noted the trashcan filled with broken playthings, but she had not seen in it the child's destructive potential. She shook her head to dispel the image.

Rachel asked, "Are you okay?"

"Yeah, fine. Sorry. It's just that when I think about this case, I start second-guessing myself, seeing things I didn't see before."

"Well, you know what they say about hindsight. I'm sure you did your best with what you had. And this girl … you're still seeing her, right? I mean, there is hope, isn't there? That she'll get better?"

Celeste didn't know what to say. The shadow swayed between them. She almost reached into it for a breadstick, then changed her mind. "I need a cigarette."

"No you don't. You need to finish telling me the story, about Annie and her family. What did she do after her dad put her mom in the emergency room?"

"Nothing at first, except withdraw further into her low-functioning, nonverbal world. Her grades were already bad. They got worse. But then she did do something. A very small act with huge consequences."

Celeste could see her friend's eyes in the candlelight, wide-open, pupils dilated, hungry for narrative—tragedy, comedy, melodrama. The human race, Celeste thought, we're all insatiable story sponges, sopping the scum of lives as we live our own, leaving new slime trails for others to absorb. A slimy mess, really. She took a sip of wine and wanted a cigarette. She wished she hadn't started this telling. Rachel's eyes made the lazy wink again. Then they both looked away.

Rachel tore off a corner of wet napkin and started rolling it into a ball. "You've got to finish this, if it's gonna do you any good. The venting, I mean. I can see it's painful for you, but that's why I'm here. You can't blame yourself for—for whatever happened. That girl ... well, she's obviously got issues, and you did what you could. She's just an emo kid, one of thousands. What could she possibly have done that's so huge, so unsettling to the natural order of things? Life will go on, hers and yours."

"But not his."

"Whose?"

"Allison's father. He's dead, remember?"

"Yeah, yeah. But you never did tell me how. What happened to him?"

"He should've never combined them, the booze and the meth. He was so distraught over the way things were going—"

"*Meth*? My God, what was he, an idiot?"

"He had no coping mechanisms, like most men. When they lose control, they get really destructive. He wasn't an idiot, really. He was just a man."

"But *meth*. I mean those people get all haggard and their cheeks sink in and their gums recede and then their teeth fall out and they look like the walking dead with their eyes dilated—"

"Yes, that does happen in extreme cases, but he hadn't got to that point yet. He started out drinking and staying out late with old buddies, trying to hide from his problems at home. He discovered meth as a way to party late and then work the next day. He was packing in as much as possible to make up for what he'd missed, or thought he'd missed, by trying to be a good husband and father. It was another way of striking back at his wife. In his warped sense of justice, destroying himself was a way of getting even."

"But he wasn't *trying* to kill himself, was he?"

"Subconsciously. Most forms of destructive behavior are symptomatic of self-loathing, guilt, shame."

"Well, sure. So did he get wasted and drive his truck off a bridge, die in a bar fight, or what?"

"No, he actually made it home safely the night he died."

"Oh. Heart attack then."

Celeste shook her head. "Nope. His death was completely painless. You could say he died in his sleep."

"That seems weird, for a man his age."

"It's weirder than you think." Celeste looked away and reached for the carafe. As she poured, filling both glasses, Allison's words flowed through her mind from that day in the office when she had finally opened up, the day that should have been a breakthrough in the case. Celeste had felt the anticipation of closing in on something—like a hunter must feel when finally flushing his prey—when Allison revealed that her father had been coming into her room at night. Celeste knew if she could get her to bring it out into the light, to talk about what her father had been doing to her, then they could begin the healing process. But the conversation took a surprising turn.

It had started with an off-hand comment that prompted Celeste to roll her chair around closer and face the girl. "What do you mean," she asked, "your father was 'acting weird' before the accident? What was he doing, besides staying out late and drinking?"

Allison's hair, long and unnaturally black, was swept across her forehead and cut in a one-sided shag. When she shook her head, the hair didn't move. "I dunno, just stuff. I don't want to talk about it."

"'Stuff' isn't very specific, Allison. I can help you get through this, but you've got to share with me. Was he being mean to you, did he ever hit you or hurt you in any way? I've got a feeling that maybe he did."

Allison looked down at her black high-top tennis shoes. She let out a short sigh of disgust. "He started coming into my room at night."

Celeste felt a wave of pity for the child. She reached out and gently touched her knee, just below a frayed hole in her tight jeans. Her voice came out soft and measured like brushes on a snare drum. "I can see how you wouldn't want your father in your room, especially at night. A girl needs some space. How would it begin, those nights when he came upstairs?"

Allison shrugged, looked away. "I dunno. He just came up. Late, after he'd been drinking. I'd hear him on the stairs and wake up."

"Wasn't that scary, being awakened in the middle of the night?"

"Sorta."

"Then what? Tell me what he would say when he came into the room, before he touched you? He did touch you didn't he? Just tell me everything. You'll feel better."

The cathartic release Celeste was expecting never came. Allison began to withdraw once again into her shadowy, silent world, picking at the holes in her jeans. When Celeste persisted in questioning her about how long it had been going on, she finally revealed that her father had only recently—since the mother's beating—begun coming upstairs to her room. "He would smell awful, and he would be all blubbery and teary eyed, telling me how much he loved me and that he would never hurt me. He would want to hug me, like I was a little girl or something."

Celeste could tell that Rachel was disappointed. "So was that it?" her friend asked. "No incest?"

Celeste shook her head.

"Well, what's so weird about that? That doesn't explain his death or why the girl is the way she is."

"I'm afraid it does. That's the problem."

"Oh my God!" Rachel said, throwing up her hands and leaning back in the booth. "Just tell the story, for Christ's sake."

Celeste raised her glass, took a long sip. "Okay. She did finally reveal enough for me to get the picture. She already hated her father for what he had done to her mother and the dogs, and she hated the way he smelled on those nights, the way he clung to her, crying. She heard him when he got home, heard the garage door go up and his truck pull inside. She lay there, dreading the sound of his foot on the stairway. But he didn't come in. She didn't hear the garage door go back down. She said she thought that maybe he had just come home to get something and was going back out. At least she hoped that was the situation. But he didn't leave and he never came into the house."

"So, you're telling me he died sitting there in his truck?"

"Exactly. The mother found him the next morning, slumped over the wheel. The ignition was on, but the engine was dead, out of gas. The coroner determined that he died of carbon monoxide poisoning, but they couldn't be sure if it was suicide or an accident. There were high levels of methamphetamine in his blood and nearly enough alcohol to kill him."

"Doesn't make sense. How was he driving? You said she heard him raise the garage door and pull inside. I don't see how he could drive home, park his truck, and then pass out in the driver's seat."

"The meth kept his system stimulated in spite of the sedative effects of the booze. Up to a point, that is. He was running on autopilot, until he got the truck inside, the gear lever in park. Then all systems failed."

Rachel wrinkled her brow, pushed her hair back. "Okay. Weird but possible, I guess. But I still don't get it. What's this got to do with the girl and the way she is?"

"She was dreading their little routine of him coming up to her room. She could hear the truck still running as she lay there waiting. Finally, she went down to see why he didn't come inside. At the bottom of the stairs there's a short hallway then the kitchen and the door that opens onto the garage. She opened the door and saw that he was passed out in the truck."

"And she just left him? That little bitch! But wait. She wouldn't have known what to do. She wouldn't have wanted to wake him."

"No." Celeste looked out into the restaurant. A busboy was clearing a table, scraping pizza remnants into a plastic garbage pan. The few customers, mostly couples, were chatting softly as they ate and sipped their wine. It was a slow night. She looked back at her friend. "She didn't want to wake him, but she did know what to do. She pressed the button and made the door go down. Then she went back to bed." Celeste watched the effect of her words on Rachel's face, the lips parting, the eyes widening. "Now you know," she said, leaning in, "why I feel like I do, why I don't know how to proceed."

After a moment Rachel said, "Oh my God. What will you do?"

Celeste shrugged. The shadow of her hands swayed and quivered over the tabletop as she poured another glass of wine.

ABOUT THE AUTHOR

RON YATES has been learning to write for most of his life. He produced good essays in high school, but his adolescent energies were largely devoted to tinkering with old cars, drag racing, drinking beer, and trying to stay out of trouble.

Although encouraged by his English teachers to pursue higher education, Yates, after graduating high school in lackluster fashion, spent time languishing in factory jobs. An aching back and a caring girlfriend prompted him to explore other options.

His enduring love of reading and nascent knack for writing guided him to a degree in English and a career teaching high school. Years later he earned an MFA in creative writing from Queens University of Charlotte.

Yates, who lives near Mt. Cheaha, on the shore of beautiful Lake Wedowee in Alabama, has published stories in a variety of journals including *Hemingway Shorts, KYSO Flash, Still: the Journal, The Oddville Press, The Writing Disorder*, and *Prime Number Magazine*. He has a son and daughter and is married to his sweetheart, Carol Yates.

Ron Yates writes about writing and other subjects at ronyates.net.

CPSIA information can be obtained
at www.ICGtesting.com
Printed in the USA
FSHW022041170319
56337FS